A Different Kind of Cheerleader

Lira
Brannon

Cypress Knoll Press Cookville, Texas
http://www.lirabrannon.com

This is a work of fiction. Names, characters, places, and incidents, either are the product of the author's imagination or are used fictitiously. Any resemblance to actual events, locales, or persons, living or dead, is entirely coincidental.

Please do not participate in or encourage piracy of copyrighted materials in violation of the author's rights. Purchase only authorized editions.

PRINTED IN THE UNITED STATES OF AMERICA

If you purchased this book without a cover, you should be aware that this book is stolen property. It was reported as "unsold and destroyed" to the publisher and neither the author nor the publisher has received any payment for this "stripped book."

This book is dedicated to athletes everywhere who have overcome.

The making of a book is never a one-man project and I want to thank all those friends and family who always believed this could happen.

In particular, I want to thank my girls, Maggie, Mollie, and Miriam who would only complain a little bit when I wanted to read the same chapter *again*.

My critique partners from NETWO who always gave such wonderful feedback—even when it hurt.

Thanks be to God for his angels, both human and heavenly.

Chapter One

"So, Tansy, have you thought about what you want to be when you grow up?"

I stared at my physical therapist, Keryn. *Had she lost her mind?* I lay prone on the mat struggling to lift a couple of puny 3-pound weights. Her concerned face hovered over my legs, long fingered hands holding them in place. Why? Because I couldn't move them, and she was all that kept me from injuring myself further while I built up the few muscles that remained.

"What?"

Something in my one-word answer must have warned her the thought of smashing her teeth in looked too tempting, because she sat back a bit.

"Well, you're thirteen; starting junior high, time to start making plans."

The olive-colored walls closed in tight around me like a too small box and the sour scent of sweaty bodies made me gag. I couldn't—no, wouldn't, think about the future. Anger, usually sleeping while I worked out with others like me, curled around my heart and twisted it into something I didn't recognize and didn't like but embraced. It served as my protection from hurtful remarks and prying physical therapists.

Ugly words tumbled from my lips in a stream I couldn't stop. "What do you mean 'make plans'? I'm a cripple. I'm stuck like this—FOREVER. I get to see you twice a week as my legs shrink away to skinny little sticks. Oh, but I forgot, you probably won't be here in a few years, you'll move on. But I won't, I'll be right here, not 'being' anything."

My voice rose to a shrill scream that reverberated off the low-slung fluorescent lights. I glared at the other three girls with their therapists at various stages of exercise. Everyone dropped their eyes—except for Meg. She ignored me completely as her stimulated legs spun the pedals of the electro bike while she jammed out on her iPod.

They obviously knew what I meant. Every day they lived half-lives like me, most just wouldn't face it. No matter where we came from, who we'd been before, we're all just cripples now. None of us had any say in the matter. I looked towards Holly and my heart hurt.

The 5-year-old cherub paused to look at me for only a moment before chattering on at the teenaged cousin who'd come to visit. She'd been standing on her front porch when the bullet from a drive-by targeted at an uncle hit her. She was still young enough to have hope. I longed for a return to that time of innocence, still believing my parents and doctors.

Like sweater dresses I'd outgrown and thrown out, hope did fit me anymore. I'd been this way since eight years old. Many paras come through here. Some have hope, some don't. Then, one by one they gave up. Never returned. And no—they never got better.

I kept my mind busy, focusing on anything but the future and the conversation Keryn wanted to have.

I zoned in on Holly's cousin, Lily, asking the same old questions at Sam, her physical therapist. "Why does Holly say she's T5 complete?"

I cringed inside. When we introduce ourselves here at physical therapy that's how we talk. I've been known to say on occasion, 'My name is Tansy and I'm a T10 incomplete'. Meg, who'd been a passenger in her boyfriend's car when he drove into a tree, would say 'I'm Meg and I have a L3 complete'. At least I think that's what she is. Meg doesn't say much. Her boyfriend used to pick her up, but he doesn't any more, and she talks evenless. That's okay though. I can see the dark monster of disappointment around her as if it were real. I know, because it's eating at me every day.

The physical therapist balanced the tiny girl on a block while she leaned over, picked up brightly colored plastic balls, and tossed them into a hat held by the overly helpful cousin.

"Well, there are four sections of the spine. Starting from the top, there are the Cervical, Thoracic, Lumbar, and Sacral." Blah, blah, blah, I wanted to plug my ears. If I pretended to be engrossed by the conversation, I could do my reps on the rubber band and ignore Keryn as she tried to catch my eye.

"The letter refers to the broken section of the spinal column. The number refers to the vertebra that actually broke. The lower it is, the more movement there is. There are complete breaks, which is where there is no feeling below the break, and incomplete, where sometimes the person can feel tingles and have a little jerky movement."

I studied Holly's face as she tossed the balls. Didn't she care that they talked like she wasn't there? As though her back was a separate being? I shook my head and released the tension band with a snap. I wanted to plug her little ears, hide her from the time when she realized that this was for real. This was all she had left and she would never walk again. That cheery, hopeful flame that burned so bright in her blue eyes would die. Her joy would fade and she would become—well—like me.

Keryn's voice pulled me unwillingly from watching the cousin nod as though she understood every word Sam said.

"Let's try the medicine ball for a while."

I slumped my shoulders to let her know I hadn't forgotten what she wanted to talk about, even though I really liked the toss game. I'd been a para since third grade, I had great upper body strength and the tossing of the weighted ball made me feel good about myself for a change.

Keryn settled me against a support block. My other physical therapist (we called them PTs) Heath, took a hold of my shoulders with a light grip. I threw the ball at Keryn—hard. I still remembered her stupid question. Instead of falling over like she had when I was a little younger, she simply caught it with a slight smile that really annoyed me. Like she meant for me to throw it that hard. I gritted my teeth and fumbled the gray sphere so that it rolled away and she had to fetch it.

So, take that.

"Just because you're in a wheelchair, doesn't mean you can't do things with your life, Tansy."

She was so not going to go there. Hadn't I made it perfectly clear that the subject was taboo? I threw the ball hard again and would have fallen over if Heath hadn't been there.

"No, I can't." I tried to pitch my voice a little lower, but it squeaked above my control. Everyone here thought it their job to push me instead of just letting me be.

Keryn didn't seem fazed by my glares. "I've read about people in wheelchairs who do all sorts of things, painters, sales people, business—"

I'd heard enough. I didn't want to be any of those things. There was only one thing that I had dreamed of being since I first saw them on TV. "I want to be a cheerleader!"

I have to hand it to Keryn, she didn't even blink. But everyone else stopped and stared at me. It must be freak show Friday and I'm the star stooge. Their thoughts were obvious. *What an idiot, wanting to be a cheerleader.* But it was true. I dreamed about it every night before I hurt my back. Every time I felt my toes tingle, or my legs started doing their spastic thing, I dared to hope that maybe my spine was healing and I would walk, despite what the doctors said. One day I'd be able to run onto the gym floor yelling and screaming with my squad. Of course, I never told anyone. It would be too embarrassing while the specialists looked anywhere but at me and tried to figure out how to tell me that would never happen.

A suspicious smell that began in the corner and wafted throughout the room saved me from answering

Keryn. Instantly all eyes turned from me to Holly. Tears leaked down her cheeks as she sniffed. "I sorry."

Her mother, one of those blonde hover types, shushed her. "It's okay, sweetie."

Sam ruffled her hair. "No worries. We'll get you cleaned up and back to work, *tout de suite*. No skipping out on me, ya hear?" Wow! French and Texan. Not a good mix.

At least people could help Holly and leave me alone. There were a few comments, but most of the girls looked away. Bowel movement bombs (BMBs we called them), were an embarrassing fact of life.

"Jees, Holly," Meg yelled, ripping the electrodes off her legs and reaching for her wheelchair. Her PT tried to help, but she pushed him away and transferred from equipment to wheels with a speed I envied.

The tall man leaned down to help adjust her legs. "Now, Meg, no need to get upset."

"Yeah? How am I supposed to work with that stink blowing everywhere? I'm outta here."

"You still have twenty minutes—"

"Just try to make me stay..."

Their voices faded away as the heavy wood door *snicked* behind them. The bleak and empty look on her face just before she turned away made me look elsewhere. Purposefully, I thought of anything but her pain. I had my own problems—like a persistent PT.

My eyes watered from the smell. Holly's mother and Sam tried to get her adjusted and to the bathroom, but it isn't like they could just rush her out like a toddler. It took a little more time and the BMB was a doozy.

I cleared my throat, trying not to think of the many times that had been me, and gave them some privacy.

"Looks like a full moon's on the rise," Heath joked over my shoulder.

Usually he could make me smile, but when I turned to Keryn, I could see she wasn't letting this go. Someone must have assigned her to talk to me. My fingers curled against my palms till the bite of fingernails drew blood. I bet it was my mom. I can just hear her. "Tansy's becoming bitter, she needs encouragement." I know her words exactly. She'd whispered them to my grandma over the phone just on Saturday.

"Can I tell you a story?"

I shrugged. "Not like I can go anywhere." She smiled and it almost made me feel guilty—almost.

"I found this on the internet the other day about the master violinist, Itzhak Perlman—"

"Not even an American."

She grinned like she expected my interruption. "Nope—Israeli. He had polio when he was a child and has to walk with braces and crutches."

I sniffed. At least he *could* walk.

But still she ignored me. "During a very important

concert, a string broke."

"So?"

"Well, playing a violin with four strings is difficult—with three almost impossible." She paused as she strapped my legs into the standing frame and stood back while Heath took up position behind me.

I pulled myself onto my feet, counted to ten, and half sat back down. I waited. She waited. She won.

"So? What happened?"

"Oh, well, he kept on playing—never missed a note, just kept making beautiful music."

I lurched upwards again. "Does this story have a point?"

"Glad you asked. When interviewed later about why he played on, instead of just stopping the music and getting a new string, his reply was "'it's the artist's task to find out how much music he can still make with what he has left.'"

"So, this is deep right, and is supposed to apply to me—how?"

Her smile tightened at the corners and her eyes narrowed. I'd hurt her, and that made me feel even worse. I didn't feel any better at making her cheery smile waver. I can't remember why it annoyed me in the first place. She really was a great PT. One of the best at the clinic. I wanted to apologize, but the words felt awkward on my tongue and wouldn't come out.

She touched my hand as I pulled myself up to stand

again. "Just because you thought you were meant to have legs, doesn't mean life is over because you don't."

I gave her my best dead eyed stare as I pulled myself up one last time. I stood in the frame, looking down at her for a full thirty seconds.

She stared right back. "Just think on it, 'kay?"

I sat back down. A beeping sound caught my attention and I motioned towards the pack on the back of my chair. It was hot pink, like my wheelchair and the stripe in my otherwise black hair. In it was everything I might need in an emergency. Some of the things were those that every kid carried around—energy bars, bottled water. Then there was the extra urine bag, a change of clothes, and of course, my phone.

"Could you hand me that?"

Keryn frowned, took a quick look around, then dug until she pulled out the slim Tracphone with the sparkly cherry sticker on the back.

"Thanks."

> Bestie: Weee'rrrree Heeerrreee
>
> I texted as fast as my numbers only phone
> would allow.
>
> Me: Where?"

> Bestie: Here girlfriend

Heath plucked the phone from my fingers and dropped it into the net pocket. "Ah, ah, ah, you know the rules—no phones during PT." He frowned at Keryn, but I was looking over their shoulders.

A face appeared in the narrow glass of the door. Long black cornrow braids with bright beads and dark purple glasses. My best friend, Bryn.

Chapter Two

I waved her in, because Bryn's shy sometimes even though she'd been to PT a lot with me over the years. She stepped through the door and stood to the side, casually chic in her white halter top with big purple flowers. A matching head scarf tied her braids into a pony tail. Jean shorts and sneakers told me she was ready for our get away to the park when we got to my house.

However, at her first breath, her face changed as the stench got sucked up her nostrils. The BMB hadn't dissipated in the closed room at all. My nose must have adjusted, but Bryn's eyes teared behind rectangle lenses. Her hand shot to her nose and she pinched it so hard her glasses tipped forward.

Blinking so fast I could almost feel the breeze, she nearly tripped over the dumbbells, not to mention Emma and Denny, her hulking physical therapist. I laughed and clapped at her performance. Just seeing her chased away all the bad feelings Keryn's conversation had dredged up.

I wheeled through the maze of equipment. "Over here, Bryn."

Removing her glasses, she squinted around the room. She'd gotten contacts for school, but she still wasn't used to them and said she hated sticking her finger in her eye— something moms all over the world yell at their kids NOT to do. "There you are. Mom sent me in to get you."

I tried to keep my smile. Squish, just like that, good mood gone. The mention of Miz Donna did that to me. I love Bryn, I do. We've been friends since before my accident, clear back to kindergarten. When my family lived next to the Winters in The Links, a gated community of five stone homes and two car garages. Our dads had worked at Preifert together in quality control. Then Bryn's dad started welding in the oil fields and pulling in the big bucks. *My* dad left because he couldn't handle a handicapped kid and Mom moved us across the highway to the North Town Trailer Park.

Now Miz Donna made it obvious every chance she got that Bryn was too good for me. It surprised me she still did a few things for my mom. Like now, picking me up when my single parent had to pull another shift at the hospital where she worked as a phlebotomist.

"Okay, I'm ready to go." I grabbed my backpack and got out of there before anyone could catch me.

Bryn hooked my bag over her shoulder and trotted down the long hall beside me. Cartoon pictures of forest animals flashed by, but I paid them no mind. I think the object is to soothe the kids going to PT, but it didn't work. When I started going, I'd been too scared to even notice the bug-eyed bunnies and three-legged deer painted by some local teen artist.

After that I was too tired, then I just didn't care. Camden, a kid that used to come, had taken a sharpie and added fangs and dripping blood to a few of the creatures. A couple he'd killed in twisted ways. He didn't come any more. Most likely he ended up at the psycho house in Terrell. He'd definitely been suicidal. Maintenance should paint over the whole thing and start over, but no one seemed to notice. Which was my point in the first place—totally forgettable.

Miz Donna, a tall woman in a flowered skirt that matched Bryn's head scarf, helped stow my chair in the back of her cherry colored minivan. I negotiated the bench seat. Bryn helped me with my legs, which she's a pro at because we've been doing this a long time. I don't know why Miz Donna has a van. Bryn's an only child. We used to have one. Now we have an older Honda civic.

"Hey, Twerp." I ducked my head into my shoulders and turned. Leo, my older brother by two years, lounged in the last bench seat. He'd slicked his black curls down in the way I hated and made his ears stand out. His brown eyes crinkled up at the corners, despite his greeting, so I couldn't tell if he was teasing. I answered the safe way. "Shut up."

Why was he here anyway? I wanted to talk to Bryn about Keryn's stupid question and tell her the story about Perlman, but no way would I talk about it with *him* in the car. He'd just laugh or make fun of it. I liked the story.

So, I asked her the question I really didn't want to, but the one I knew she was waiting for. "So, how'd it go?"

Bryn turned so suddenly and with such a wide grin on her face, I cringed. *Oh boy, here it comes.* "It went super!" Oh my goodness, she practically gushed out the words. "The kids were perfect angels. Everyone worked so hard—they all knew their lines—even Jayda. The play went off without a hitch. Sarah was so cute..." Bryn had been helping all week at her church's Vacation Bible School with the first and second graders and she couldn't talk enough about her kids.

Thank goodness that ended today.

As she rambled on about the play, something about Jesus making his grand entrance. I smiled and nodded. Bryn had been saved while at some expensive church camp at the beginning of summer. She is my best friend, sure, but sometimes I couldn't stand the way she had become a Jesus freak. Every conversation was Jesus this and Jesus that. Her mother had been in a fender bender not too long ago and then the rants became all about guardian angels.

Me? I don't want anything to do with the Man who let me fall and break my back. As for guardian angels, they must have been sleeping on the job at the park that day, because one didn't catch me. Then, of course, my dad left, and we had to move.

Nope. I don't want to know what God has in mind for me because, as far as I'm concerned, his plans suck.

Miz Donna dropped us off at my house, with a small sniff at Mister Santi. He sat in his boxers and tee shirt in his favorite drab green lawn chair. A sweetish smell wafted into the narrow street, overpowering the odor of bacon grease and rotted fruit from the dumpster two trailers down.

He leaned forward as we opened the doors of the van and waggled his fingers at Bryn's mom. "*Venir aquí, señora bonita.*" You didn't have to know Spanish to get his meaning.

Leo grabbed my wheelchair, handed it off to Bryn, and headed up the ramp without a backwards glance. Miz Donna dove back into the front seat, barely giving me time to close the door before the red van sped off and whipped around in the dead end. She leaned out the window. "One hour, Brynley, and you stay away from that man."

"Yes, Mom. Can we walk to the park?"

I could tell her mom didn't want my bestie anywhere around my home, but old habits are hard to break. "As long as you're home by five." She took off like Mister Santi would actually come down off his porch and talk to her. We'd lived here four years. In all that time I'd only seen him sit in the chair or disappear inside.

We turned back to the house and I sighed in disgust. The metal siding had faded in the harsh Texas sun to the washed-out color of concrete. The skirting, new last spring, blinded the eyes and made the siding look even worse. A gaping hole near the end gave the house a snaggle-tooth appearance. Around Christmas, one of the pipes had frozen and burst, flooding underneath. The plumber left it open to dry, but he never came back to put the panels up. Mom had been a little late with the payment.

A ramp (built by some do-gooder association when the accident first happened) led to a small covered deck shading the front porch. The rails split and warped—wood did that in Texas. I wanted to paint it (hot pink, of course). Mom says, "we'll see."

Window air conditioners hung limply out every window in sight, and dripping water like snot running out of a toddler's nose.

17

Bryn doesn't seem to see this. She skipped up my ramp. "Come on. I'm starving. I bet you are too, even if you can't feel it."

This is true. Sometimes I don't know when my body is hungry because all the signals got confused when my spine broke. It was Bryn's nice way of reminding me I should get something to munch on. She's cool that way.

Bryn went ahead and opened the door. She put her shoulder into it because the bottom tended to drag on the linoleum squares where the house shifted. It opened with a bang against the edge of the couch. I'm an expert at maneuvering through the smallish hole.

Mom stood in the kitchen, cutting apples and cheese. Leo pigged out at the table, but Bryn shouldered in and snagged one for me.

"How was PT?"

I shrugged. "Same ol', same ol'." The apples tasted good, stimulating my hunger button at last. "Holly's cousin, Lily, was there."

Mom nodded. "That's nice, anything else?"

I stared at her hard, wondering if she *had* put Keryn up to talking to me. "Holly had a BMB."

Bryn raised her eyebrows at me; she knew what I was talking about. I hid a grin when Mom asked. "BMB?"

"You know, bowel movement bomb."

Leo tossed down his apple slice. "Come on! Do we have to talk about this when we're eating?"

"Wimp."

Mom handed Bryn a small cup of caramel for dipping her apples and gave me "the look". The food effectively turned Leo's attention. He protested favoritism towards the visitor, but it was different when he looked at Bryn and took a swipe at it. She moved it towards me. She'd been around my brother a long time and knew that food needed to be kept out of his reach or it disappeared. Still, the smile on his face was one I hadn't seen in a long time.

Jealously pinched me. "Are we still shopping during tax free weekend, Mom?" It had become tradition that when the beginning of a new school year neared, we would get clothes and supplies during the weekend Texas suspended the sales tax. We always had loads of fun.

Mom put the peanut butter on the counter. Peanut butter on anything was one of my favorites.

"I almost forgot that's this weekend."

I eyed her as I slathered more peanut butter than apple on my snack and tried to gauge if she truly had forgotten or she didn't have the money for it. "But sure. Of course, we'll go. I'll need to take a little nap in the morning. Plan on two o'clock." Relief flooded me. It had just slipped her mind is all.

I looked at Bryn and she nodded. "That sound's great, Miz Lisa."

I met her eyes "The usual?"

She grinned. *"Burnes* it is."

I envisioned heaps of clothes in mismatched piles just waiting to be dug through. Almost as much fun as Goodwill.

Leo rolled his eyes. "I don't know how you guys can stand that place. It's such a mess." This from a boy who hadn't seen his bedroom floor in months.

Bryn started peeling a tangelo. "You find the best deals in the piles. Remember those tank tops I found? Three of them on one hanger, for one price!"

I grinned. "Yeah, then Mr. Tredloe told you they were against school dress code and had you put on a sweater."

She shrugged. "They were good for layering, anyway." Bryn liked layers and had a flair for making the most unlikely matches look great. "I hope we can find some clothes in our new school colors for spirit week."

"Me too. White, black, and gold are much more interesting than purple and white."

"Ohh, and some hair ties too."

"And Mom, we need sparklies!" I added.

Mom laughed. "Okay, we'll look for glitz."

"But only in black and gold," said Bryn. "Cheerleaders have to have spirit all the time. Not just on the court and at games."

I gagged and coughed up bits of apple. Just the mention of cheerleading made my throat tighten.

Bryn pounded my back. "You okay?"

Mom handed me a glass of water. "Slow down, Tansy."

Everything about the afternoon and the talk with Keryn came back. Was it a conspiracy?

I raised my eyebrow and stared at my mom. Then it hit me. Oh...my...gosh—my diary. My heart lurched when I thought about it laying on the bed, in the open, available for anyone to read.

"I'll be right back."

Bryn and Leo ignored me, but Mom searched my face. I hated the way she always seemed to look right into my center. Had she been reading my diary? I wheeled down the hall all the way to the end of the trailer and the big room that looked out over the street. My diary sat exactly where I'd left it.

> *Dear Diary*
>
> *I guess that's what I'm supposed to start with. Even if this is a stupid journal my shrink, oh, excuse me, counselor, told me to start. Mom took me to her because everyone says I'm being cranky. 'Course Leo calls it something else behind Mom's back. The counselor says I'm bitter. Who me? What do I have to be bitter about? I'm just welded to this wheelchair for the rest of my life. But they can't understand that, no, they expect me to act like*

everything is normal. But, how can I? The only thing I ever wanted to do was cheer with Coach Angel's squad when I reached junior high. Junior high starts in three days, and tryouts are in six. Bryn will try out, and I'll watch, just like always. Me? Bitter? Naw.

It's strange that the very thing Keryn brought up in her conversation was the exact thing I had written about this morning. My eyes narrowed as a suspicion sneaked into my brain. Were they all talking about me behind my back?

I tucked the journal under my blanket. I love Bryn, but I didn't want to talk about it. I'd even listen to her preach to avoid thinking about all the things I'd never get to do. "Let your feelings out." Mom had said when she sent me to my room to write this morning. She used that sickly-sweet voice reserved for when she asked me to do something I didn't want to do. Or when I became too difficult to handle and she was counting down from ten in her head like the counselor had told her to do. Maybe it's Mom that needed to see the shrink. Not me.

"Tansy," Mom called down the hall, "did you forget Bryn was here?"

"Of course not! I'm taking care of personal stuff." I yelled back. Those were words that would give me as much time as I needed to do whatever. No one wanted to barge in on a cripple trying to change a urine bag.

I checked it anyway and then reached for the diary again. I tore out a paper and wrote: *It's the artist's task to find out how much music he can still make with what he has left.*

I liked it. I dug in my desk until I found a tack and stuck it on the wall. Right at my eye level, waist high for most people. After everything and everybody getting on me today, it still made the most sense. Perhaps it was the only thing that did. For some reason the words made me think that there might be something for me.

Chapter Three

I nearly ran over Leo in the hall.

"Watch it!" he growled. I smirked and cut the wheels across his bare toes. He yelped and leapt back, but no way would he complain to Mom while Bryn was around. I think he kind of liked her. That ticked me off even more.

I barreled down the hall and whipped into the kitchen. "Hey, sorry."

Bryn pushed her glasses up her nose. "No problem. You ready to go?"

Mom paused in washing the cutting board. "Where you two headed?"

I rolled my eyes at Bryn, but the other girl seemed to

shrink. "The skate park, of course." *Edwards* was the only park within wheeling distance. It came complete with handicapped swings and a cemetery next to the basketball court. But the thing that made my mom pale was the tube and rails of the skate park.

I hate how the color in my mother's face drained whenever I mentioned it. Not like I could go skateboarding and break my back *again*. I glared at my mother's worried eyes and stuck out my jaw. Of course, it was childish, but I wasn't going to let her ruin this one little bit of freedom I had. And if I didn't mind going to the park where this whole thing had started, Mom could just get over it.

She should have moved us if it was going to bug *her* for the rest of *her* life.

Finally, Mom dropped her eyes. "Just be careful."

Leo flipped up the skateboard by the back door and grabbed his helmet off the rack. "I'm going too, Mom. Be back in an hour or so." *She never worries about him and he even gets to skateboard.*

Goody two-shoes, always trying to show me up. He usually oozed sweetness right after mom and I faced off. I wrinkled my lip at him when Mom turned away.

"All right. Dinner is microwave mac and cheese. Just stick it in for a few minutes."

Leo waved. "Got it."

Mom glanced at me, smiled, and hurried off to her

bedroom to change into scrubs. She pulled the night shift at the hospital this quarter and would be in the lab all night.

When we were clear outside, I bumped my castor wheels on Leo's Achilles tendon. "I wish you wouldn't do that."

"Hey, quit—that hurts!" Leo rubbed his injury and glared at me. "Do what?"

"Be all sweet and everything. You're just faking it."

My brother shrugged then sneered. "I just keep it real. You've got to make a big issue out of everything. Like anyone even cares that you broke your back at the park anymore. We'd forget too, if you'd just let us."

Such a liar. Was he blind? Mom nearly freaked out whenever we went.

Tears stung at my eyes. I gave my chair a big push to catch my friend. I didn't want to give him the satisfaction of making me cry. Bryn focused straight ahead, trying to catch a glimpse of the people at the park just over the hill. "Sorry." I mumbled, embarrassed to have made her feel uncomfortable.

She quirked her lips at me. "S'okay."

"You alright?"

"Yeah."

Before, even just a few months ago, Bryn would break out in a sweat and start to shake when people argued. Not like she did it all the time, but it was obvious to me.

"You're pretty cool about it. That's different." I didn't like the look she slanted at me. She hesitated, like she didn't want to say something, and my heart leaped. What would my best friend *not* want to say to me?

"I *am* different. At least I hope I am. Jesus saved me at camp this year." Questions spun crazy in my mind. What exactly did that mean? She'd told me that before, but why would that make her not be upset when people started to fight? And it wasn't just that, although that was a biggie, she didn't get as snarky about some of the girls from last year we had fun talking about. And Jesus showed up in just about every conversation. As though my silence encouraged her, she went on. "Jesus helps me keep my cool when I feel like I'm getting tense."

Jealousy washed over me and the heat I felt wasn't from the Texas sun. "Like a friend?"

"Kind of. I start praying when the shakes come and then there's just peace. Like all the knots inside me have been let loose."

I didn't want to talk about knots. I had so many I felt like a friendship bracelet made by a 4-year-old. But I liked them, they were mine, and I didn't need anyone untying them. Looking ahead to the park, I searched for a distraction.

"I heard Jyme say he was going to be here this afternoon." It worked. Bryn's eyes sparkled. I sighed in relief. If anything would get my bestie's attention off Jesus, it was the mention of the boy she'd had a crush on since we were ten. Now we were thirteen, she melted every time he walked by.

"That's what he said." I giggled at her breathless whisper and she punched my arm, her voice lowered. "Well, if Jyme is there, so is Jamie." My hand slipped on the wheel at the mention of Jyme's identical twin, nearly giving me a rubber burn. Bryn saw it and grinned, but I shook my head, smashing the little butterflies that had taken flight in my stomach. Could I be hungry again? I had no right thinking of boys. For that matter, what boy would think of me?

I cleared my throat. "So, what? We need to find a place for you to practice your moves for tryouts."

Bryn's grin grew until she looked like a shark. "You brought it up."

I coasted down the little hill leading to the park, trying to ignore the way my breath got stuck in my throat when I saw the tubes, stairs, and rails where the kids of the neighborhood gathered on summer evenings. It was hard not to look at the sidewalk that led to it. That small stretch of pavement where the accident occurred had changed my life. But like a magnet, my eyes were drawn to it.

It'd been such a simple, stupid thing. One minute I was playing on Leo's skateboard (with a helmet on even), when wham, I was flat on my back on a curb, unable to move. Just a small break, the doctors said, an incomplete, but it was enough. Here I was, glued to this sweltering chair for the rest of my life. That little break had ruined everything in an instant. Dad left, Mom had to work all the time, Leo hated me, and my dream of being a cheerleader, well, of doing anything, vanished like desserts around my brother.

"Tansy?"

I hurried to where Bryn waited under a spreading oak. She leaned on a chain of a handicapped swing watching the boys. Some high schoolers tried sliding down the rail, falling and laughing while a more serious teenager looped silently back and forth in the tube.

She nudged me. "He's here."

A skinny kid in ripped jeans and baggy tee tried to jump a curb. His board went sliding out from under him, but he landed perfectly balanced on his feet. If only I'd been able to do that.

"Woot whoo!" Bryn's yell nearly split my ear drum. Jyme looked up and nodded her way. I undid the hook that chained the handicapped swing and wheeled my chair on. Bryn settled into a regular swing the next section over where we could watch the boys and still look like we were doing something *other* than watching boys. Bryn became so engrossed she forgot to give me a push. Shrugging, I locked my brakes and tried to get the swing rocking. The one I'd chosen was pretty heavy though and didn't want to move in this heat either.

"Need a hand?"

Jyme's twin, Jamie, leaned over from behind. He must have been at the table on the other side of the massive oak. Probably had a book too.

My tongue stuck to my teeth and when I opened my mouth to answer, I sounded like an idiot. "Uh, sure."

He pulled back and let go. The swing rocked gently. I looked back over my shoulder and frowned, letting Jamie know exactly what I thought of his "push". He grinned and his eyebrows lowered at my challenge. He grabbed hold of the chains again. This time the heavy air moved. Wind brushed my face, cooling the sweat that dripped from my temples and beaded embarrassingly on my upper lip. I closed my eyes and raised my face to the sky. Enjoying the free feeling for just a moment. Then, like always, the weight of the heavy metal platform slowed the swing to a stop. My ride over before it really began.

Jamie walked around the swing, studying it. I tried to shrink down in my chair.

"You just can't keep the kinetic energy up."

I forgot trying to disappear and stared at him. "What?"

"You have to have someone push or you'll stop," he explained.

I stared at him. Well, duh, but that didn't strike me as the thing to say to a super cute guy.

He tossed a book in my lap. "Here. Hold this." Then he jumped behind me again, pushing hard and high. I held my hands out and let the breeze tickle the space between my fingers. I imagined myself a bird flying, free of this stupid chair and platform swing. I was a cheerleader sailing high in a toss. For a moment that ugly feeling that always seemed to be clutching at my heart eased and I could take a deep breath. I knew it couldn't last long, but Jamie kept pushing and pushing. It rated as one of the longest swings I'd had in a forever. He outlasted Bryn by several minutes. While he pushed, that lightness stayed with me.

Then my brother's annoying voice butted in from the skate park. "Hey, Jamie! You coming?"

The swing slowed.

"Yeah, just a minute." Jamie dashed to the tree and palmed the edge of his board with a kick. He started towards the others.

"Hey, your book!" I glanced up at the title as I shook it above my head. *Fun Physics Projects for Tomorrow's Rocket Scientists? Really?* Jamie didn't say a thing, just grabbed the book and stuffed it in his backpack.

"Thanks." I called after him.

Halfway across the grass, he turned back with a quick wave and a smile before rushing over to my frowning brother. I turned to Bryn. Where had she been this whole time?

She sat on her swing, hands clamped over her mouth. Her eyes bugged behind her glasses and she snorted over her fingers.

"Don't you dare laugh." I warned her.

She snickered anyway. "'You just can't keep the kinetic energy up.' He really said that," she mumbled through her fingers. Then she couldn't keep it in any longer and began barking like a coyote. "That's the worst line I've ever heard!"

"Shhh. He'll hear you!" If I thought I'd been hot before, now my face burned like fire.

She doused her snickers, but her grin remained. She kicked off the swing. "Let's go practice our moves. No one's on the basketball court."

"Course not. It's too hot." But I undid the chain and released my brakes to back off the swing while Bryn steadied the front. I didn't want to go. We played at being cheerleaders when no one was looking, but in just a few days, Bryn would actually try out, while I would just be playing.

Still, I followed her. She was my best friend after all. "The boys are boring anyway."

I shouldn't have said that, it just made her giggle again. "Wanna race over there?"

I laughed at her suggestion. "You're too slow!" Would she do it? Actually, race against me, knowing she'd lose? With boys around? Once upon a time she'd jump at the chance, Bryn's long legs made her one of the fastest girls in elementary school. But in this one thing I had the advantage, two tires and two hands. She just had two legs.

My friend's smile widened, and she took off like a rabbit in the high beams of a car. For a moment I let her run, she hadn't failed me. Should I let her win? Not a chance. I slicked my hands across the tires and raced down the path while she cut across the thick Bermuda grass. It might be close, but no way could she out distance me.

I skidded onto the basketball court with only a half second to spare. Bryn executed a stunning round-off back handspring. My inner mantra began immediately. *Don't be jealous, do not be jealous. Say something nice. Anything!* That chant that came into my head whenever my bestie did something that made me want to scream in frustration. I wanted so bad to leap up and join her.

"Hey, Girl, you got flava!" I finally yelled. Proud that not even a bit of disappointment showed. Bryn had definitely improved over the summer. Tryouts were in the bag for her. My problem was, even though I'd been stuck in this contraption for almost as long as my memories, we'd dreamed of cheering—together. Now Bryn would move on. I never would.

Bryn ran over with another cartwheel and slid down into the splits. She rolled over on the crinkly, brown grass right next to a mound of red dirt.

"Watch out for those fire ants."

"Ow, yeah." She picked the head off a Dallisgrass and plucked at the seeds, trying to catch her breath in the heavy heat. "Okay, girl, let's see what you've got."

I couldn't help grinning. Mom would kill me if she saw me goofing around like this. I'd taken a few tumbles when first learning to maneuver my chair. Nothing bad, more embarrassing really, especially with Leo around to make the most of them. But it scared Mom half to death. She had anti-tip bars installed and everything. A quick look around confirmed no one nearby, boys busy with the boards and half hidden by a line of blooming crepe myrtles. No cars on the road.

I picked up speed on the slight slope. Two hard pushes were all it took. At the half court line, I grabbed one wheel with my gloved hand and spun once. I flourished both arms like an Olympic gymnast.

Of course, my most fervent supporter clapped and whistled. "That's what I'm talkin' about—you look like an ice skater when you do that. Next thing, you'll be doing a triple lutz like on that movie."

"Ha ha—you're too funny. Besides, didn't she go blind or something? That's all I need."

For a moment, we just let the little bit of wind cool us, but I could tell there was something on Bryn's mind. Usually when we sat like this she could be still like a statue. Kind of weird really. But today she twisted her fingers, pushed back her hair, shoved her glasses up, brushed at grass on her knee, and flicked a fire ant. All within a minute.

"Okay—so give. What's up?"

Bryn stared off towards the boys, and for the second time that day she wouldn't meet my eyes. "Well, you know school starts Monday."

I nodded, my traitorous tongue stuck to the top of my mouth so I couldn't say anything again. Seventh grade at Mt. Peaceable Junior High. Bigger school, new people to stare at me and ask questions—or worse, stare and not ask the questions they really wanted to. The people assuming just because I was in a wheelchair, they had to lean in close and yell. And of course, the new teachers I had to break in. They always wanted to help, and that made me stand out even more.

Bryn didn't seem to notice my silence. She went on. "Then tryouts are just a few days later."

Of course, I knew. Two days to be exact. Wednesday at 3:00 sharp in the gym. Hadn't we been counting down to this since kindergarten?

"I think you should try out for the Angels."

Whoa! Didn't see that one coming. My breath rushed out of my lungs and it seemed like I couldn't get enough air. "You what?" Had Bryn hit her head during practice when I wasn't looking? It was cool having a friend who didn't treat me like an invalid all the time, but could she really forget that I came in a package with this rubber and metal jigsaw puzzle? I didn't. No, I remembered every minute of every day.

How could she be so cruel? Tears stung my eyes, but no way would I cry. "Yeah, sure thing, Bryn. You are so *not* nice." I turned my chair to go.

Bryn grabbed an armrest and I stared down at her hand. *Really?* This was not like my friend at all. "No, wait." Her words rushed out in a stream, each ripping at me like arrows from her lips. "I didn't mean to make you cry. You can just do so many cool tricks with that thing that I thought, why not?"

I slapped at her hand. "Because I can't jump, or kick, or hold anyone up, Dummy." How could she even bring this up? We'd been friends for so long. And she wasn't just talking about the cheer squad that went to the football games—she was talking about the Angels. The competition squad. The baby of the star cheer coach, Coach Angel (thus the name). Each year she chooses a special set of girls to compete against other school cheer squads. Ever since the beginning of the program, three years now, they had been 2nd once and 1st twice.

It made no sense for Bryn to even suggest such a stupid thing. We'd been friends for too long. She knew exactly what I could and couldn't do. But she wasn't giving up. "Don't be dense. Your arms aren't broke. You can wave pom poms and clap. Everyone in the trailer park and my neighborhood knows you can yell."

I yanked the tire away from the other girl's grip. "Get off me! I thought we were tight. I thought you were different and you understood. But you're just like everyone else. Always wanting me to push myself, better myself. You have some great advice for me too? You gonna tell me I'm too angry, that I need to plan for the rest of my life?"

Bryn leaned over me, not backing down like usual when I raised my voice. Where did this new confidence come from? I didn't like it—not one bit. She wouldn't give up. "Don't be so touchy, Tansy. And you *are* angry. All the time. Always yelling at people. Why not be a cheerleader? You shouldn't give up on your dream just because you're in a wheelchair. You'll just be a little different is all. Think of all the fun we'd have. I know you could do it. It would be so cool. Just like we always wanted." She put her other hand on my shoulder. "Please, think about it. God doesn't want you to give up on everything, and neither do I."

Ohh, she was good. She must have rehearsed this speech in front of the mirror. Everything was perfect, the pleading in her eyes, I think I even saw a glint of tears. But I can't believe the things that were coming out of her mouth. How could she say that to me? Me of all people?

"God! You get God out of this conversation right now, Bryn, or we're through. He's the one that put me in this chair. He's the one that made me different. He's why I can't be a cheerleader. I already stand out. I don't need MORE people staring at me. I'd just be stupid looking.

Look at the poor invalid trying to be 'normal'."

Bryn got that look on her face that told me more was coming, and I knew I wasn't going to like it. "You're not stupid, and you've got some really cool moves. When I told Coach Angel she said—"

"You talked to Coach about me?" I screamed. *Of all the double crossing, back biting—*

"Of course, I did. Mom and her are friends and we went to *Diddy's* the other day. I told you, we're in this together. I learned at camp that with Jesus in your life you can do anything, and I've seen it. For real, Tansy. Mom was protected in the accident. I don't get so scared when people get angry any more. He's helped me in so many ways. I know that if you just let Him, He'd help you too."

I gritted my teeth so hard my fillings squeaked. "I told you to leave your religious stuff out of this, Bryn. I don't want nothing to do with it." A quick left-handed push and I spun my chair out of her grasp. The pavement whizzed by as I picked up speed on the sidewalk. I didn't have to look at the skate park to know that the boys were staring. How could they not with all the yelling going on and Bryn blubbering all alone. But I didn't care! I wouldn't care! Everyone was ganging up on me today!

Behind me, I thought maybe Leo yelled as I skidded into the parking lot and toward the road. I just needed to get home, away from all the eyes. I didn't see the car, but I heard it honk as I cut across the driveway and headed to the trailer park. Thank goodness for downhill. By the time I got home, I shook all over and sweat saturated my clothes. I had pushed my body too hard.

Chapter Four

Mom looked up from finishing off the apples when I slammed through the door. I grumbled as I turned my back to it and hit it three or four times to get through. She started away from the sink and rushed over to me. My legs jumped and jerked uncontrollably with spastic twitches. I yanked off my gloves and pushed down on my knees. *Stop it!* Pain began a steady *thump, thump, thump* along my arms and ribs. My face and hands burned.

"What's wrong, Tansy? You're drenched." She grabbed an ice pack from the freezer and a cool rag and started wiping at my face like I was a baby.

I batted her hand away. "Stop it." I wanted to go to

my room. I needed to get away from her, from everybody. But my arms draped like spaghetti noodles across the armrests and my hands wouldn't grip the wheels. Mom hovered. I just wanted to be alone. I couldn't leave, so I buried my face in my hands and hid.

Mom's breath rushed out. "Aww, Baby." Her arms wrapped around my shoulders, strong and cool in her long-sleeved scrubs. I tried to shake her off, she was just going to make me cry. She held on. I couldn't stop the sobs then, so I turned into her shoulder and cried. Maybe I was a baby. A big wheelchair bound infant.

Mom rocked my shoulders and murmured nonsense that felt so good against my temple and on my boiling feelings. When was the last time we hugged? She was always touching me, helping me, lifting me, washing me. But hugging? I wrapped my arms around her and sobbed even harder.

I ricocheted between rage and despair—frustration and helplessness. I couldn't tell which one made me cry. Seemed like everybody had ganged up on me today. Keryn, Bryn, and of course God. He was all mixed up in this somehow too. Mom pulled away when the snotty hiccups started. I took the cool rag she proffered, then cuddled my cheek against the ice pack.

"You want to tell me what happened?"

I glanced at the clock on the microwave. "You'll be late."

She shrugged. "I called and said I'd be in at seven." Guilt added to my other aches and I almost started crying again. Unable to meet her eyes, I looked at my lap. She'd stayed to make sure we'd make it home okay. We probably couldn't afford it.

It made me feel like I owed her somehow. "Bryn and I had a fight."

Mom stepped to the fridge and poured me a tall glass of juice. "Why? Everything seemed okay when you guys left."

"Just everything, Mom. She's changed a lot." I sipped the orange juice. It hit my taste buds like an electric charge. My stomach clenched, telling my brain, finally, that I needed a drink. I guzzled the cool liquid until the juice dribbled down my chin and brain freeze set in.

Mom looked pointedly at the rag. "Slow down, Tansy. Good changes?"

Were they good? "Well, no, I don't think so. She argues with me. She never did that before."

"Argues? That is different for Bryn, but even friends have differences. What did you argue about?"

I bit my lip and looked out the tiny kitchen window. Oak pollen from the spring still clung in sticky, yellow swirls. "She wants me to try out for the Angels."

I expected her to start protesting how dangerous it was. How I might get hurt, tipped over, stepped on, whatever. But she was quiet for a long time. Still, I didn't look away from the swirls. Patterns formed. A skateboard took shape, maybe a tube of lipstick, and—no way—a wheelchair? That's just sick, being a para had really twisted my imagination.

When Mom didn't speak, I looked at her. She didn't seem shocked. No anger at my friend being such a jerk either.

"Why shouldn't you?"

What was with everyone today? This was my mom here, afraid of every little bump. "What do you mean? Look at me, Mom. I'm not exactly cheerleader material."

"I see you, Dear. I always have. You've wanted to be a cheerleader ever since you were little and if it's what you want to do, I think you should go for it." Now I knew she'd read that journal entry. Just one stupid little note to myself and everybody gets in on a huge conspiracy against me.

"How did you know I wanted to be a cheerleader?"

Mom's lips quirked, but her eyes stayed sad. "Come on, Tansy. You've danced in front of the TV since the moment you could pull yourself up."

That little flicker of hope that might have sparked in my thoughts—got squashed. Yeah, she remembered back to the time where I could pull myself up onto two feet. Not me now. "Look at me, Mom." Maybe if I screamed, I could make her actually see me. I was a foot shorter and two feet wider than everyone else.

Mom's eyes bored into me. "I see a strong girl that can do anything she sets her mind too. Even being a cheerleader."

"Aren't you afraid I'd hurt myself? Do something stupid? Embarrass you?"

Mom turned away. "Sometimes."

"Sometimes?"

With a deep breath she turned back. "Sometimes I worry that you'll hurt yourself. But kids have to grow that way. I'd be happier seeing you doing something you love rather than moping in your room." She touched my head. "And you'll never embarrass me, Tansy, ever. I have to go. Do you need my help to clean up before I head to work?"

Before I could answer, the door slammed against the wood arm of the sofa and Leo stormed in. "What's going on? You about got hit back there!" I ducked. *Tattletale.* I scooted towards my room—fast.

As I rolled into my room, the phrase I'd tacked up caught my eye. —*it's the artist's task to find out how much music he can still make with what he has left.* That's me alright. Leftovers. I got ready for my shower by inching out of my clothes and starting the twice daily ritual of looking for any red spots or sores on my body.

The thing with sitting in a chair all day, especially on

the hot ones, is that certain parts get rubbed raw. That could mean big problems for a para. A red spot meant that I need to keep pressure off that area, move around more, that sort of thing. A little redness could quickly turn into a huge ulcer if ignored.

When I first broke my back and wasn't as mobile, I'd gotten a few pressure sores. One on my heel from where it dragged on the floor when I transferred from place to chair. Then I got one on my butt. Taking care of that had been embarrassing. There are some places you just can't reach very well alone. Mom used to do the inspection for me, but I took it over when I could.

Once done, I shrugged into my favorite lime green robe and headed for the shower. I tried not to think of Bryn and our fight. It was becoming a habit, I realized, not thinking about the things that upset me. This thought made me uncomfortable, made me think that maybe people were right about me. A thought which I immediately quit thinking about. *Ohhh, I'm good at that.*

I opened the door and found Leo standing on the other side. "What do you want?"

He looked down at the brown shag carpet. His hair curled where the heat had melted the gel. I liked it better that way, like when we were kids. "Just checking on you. You took off pretty fast and Mom was worried. She had to leave for work, so I told her I'd check on you."

I choked back the smart mouth answer that leapt to

my lips and nodded. He told Mom he'd do it, but he didn't have to actually follow through. I looked up at him, glad that the sun was setting. Shadows lurked on his face and mine. We could be anyone standing here in this pokey old hall barely wide enough for my wheelchair. A normal brother and sister. I could just be sitting in a chair, instead of dependent on it. Not headed to the bathroom that had been remodeled by removing his closet so I could have a specially designed shower.

Tears pricked at the corner of my eye, ready to break free at any show of kindness. He'd grown a lot this last year, I think, even though he hunched down a bit to talk to me. I cleared my throat. "I'm okay."

"I warmed up the mac and cheese and put the bacon bits on the counter."

"Thanks."

"I'm gonna play *Immortality* for a while." He shuffled stepped into his room and shut the door in my face. I stared after him, trying to figure him out. *Brothers—who knew?*

The tinkling tune of my phone greeted me after my shower. I hurried over, knowing without looking Bryn had texted. I turned the phone end over end, putting off reading the message. We'd never really fought before. Bryn is always so easy going about everything. My hand paused on the phone as a thought burst into my head. She used to be easy going, always letting me have my way with everything. Was that the cause of our arguments now? Bryn refusing to do things my way?

I sat on the bed and fingered the cherry sparkle sticker. She'd given it to me at my first phone christening. I'd wanted a hot pink phone with all the features. But TracFones didn't come in colors and a smart phone was way out of Mom's budget. So, Bryn gave me the sticker to dress up the phone and make me feel better.

I turned it over to read the text.

Bestie: Hey, BFF, you there?

I loved the way she called me that. *We were best friends, weren't we?* Even if now she was saved (from what I still couldn't figure). That same old anger I felt every time I thought of God flushed through me, but I pushed it down. What had Mom said? Even besties could have differences. God was just going to have to be one of those.

I looked at the clock. She'd texted around the time I headed for the shower. A cold sweat broke out on me, though the air conditioner thundered full blast right beside me. What if she thought I was ignoring her? What if she thought I really didn't want to be friends anymore? None of that was true, of course, despite what I'd said at the park. She shouldn't keep pushing God down my throat, though, I needed to make that clear. Although there many words needed to be said, and "I'm sorry" probably should have been one of the first, I thumbed a one-word answer.

Me: Hey.

Was she gone? Had she given up waiting for me? The seconds ticked by.

Bestie: Sorry.

How could she say that so easily?

Me: Yeah, me too.

Bestie: We still on for shopping tomorrow?"

I snorted.

Me: Like a little tiff is going to get in the way of shopping. This IS junior high. ;-)

I could see her pushing her glasses up as she smiled.

Bestie: That's right!

Me: Come over early?

Bestie: Can't. Mom says I have to clean my room or I can't go. :-(

Me: Need help?

Bestie: You know it.

Mom wouldn't mind me being out of the house while she slept. She didn't like me crossing the highway on my own though. Maybe Leo would take me.

Me: I'll be over if I can get Leo up.

Bestie: Ok. See you then.

Me: Yep.

Bestie: Just one more thing. Phil 4:13.

Think on it. :)

I stared at the screen. What was that? What was she trying to say? I'd never seen that before. And what did she mean? Think on it. I turned it this way and that. Was it a keyboard emoticon? Disgusted, I tossed it on the bed, too proud to ask what she meant. Maybe I'd ask tomorrow. I suspected it had to do with her religion and that ticked me off. I'd wait, cool down, then see. That seemed the best idea.

Chapter Five

The next day I couldn't get Leo out of bed before noon, so I didn't get to help Bryn clean her room. My phone stayed bright with the constant texting. True to her word, Mom shuffled from her bedroom and got ready to go when she said. The battered Civic pulled into Bryn's at exactly two. She waited just inside, keeping an eye out, and ran to the car when it pulled through the iron gates.

The first thing on the list? *Burnes*. The huge warehouse with miles of racks stretching front to back just waited with hidden treasure waiting to be discovered. They have jewelry, shoes, toys, every opportunity to find the perfect bargain. Usually the store had a church-like atmosphere, rather quiet and semi-organized. But on tax-free weekend that all changed. Mothers towing toddlers, tweens, teenagers, aunts, grandmothers, and sometimes desperate single fathers, pawed through the racks, rearranging and throwing clothes into disarray. Resolute sales people tried to keep up, but clothes ended up in great big piles in waist high bins. Bryn and I loved this treasure hunting time of year.

The men's section, on the other hand, lay like a deserted island. Leo browsed for a few minutes, found a couple of T-shirts, a pair of jeans, and tennis shoes, all in the time it took Bryn and me to get through the displays at the front.

He waved at Mom. "I'm headed to *Hastings*. See ya there."

She nodded and watched him go. Lately he'd been telling her he was doing something instead of asking. I could tell it bugged her and her thoughts were cooking up ways to talk to him about it.

I shrugged and wheeled into the battle. On days like this, with hands grasping and clothes disappearing right in front of my nose, Bryn used me unashamedly. No one wants to get in the way of the kid in the wheelchair, or take something just out of her reach. Bryn pushed me to a huge bin, separating two gray haired women, and we started digging.

She flourished a skirt. "I've found it!"

I eyed the little thing. "It's kind of short."

She held the hanger at arm's length and squinted. She had in her contacts today, trying to get ready for school and they were making her eyes tired. Maybe that's why she couldn't see the shortness of the white, black, and gold plaid skirt.

"No," she finally decided. "It's fabulous. And it's the perfect colors for our school. It will be great for the day of tryouts, don't you think?" She fingered the black elastic belt stretching from the middle of each side and ending in black, patent leather ends with gold buckles. "Just right. But it's missing something."

I grinned. "I thought you said it was perfect."

"It is." She snatched a matching one from under a gray hair lady's reaching fingers and flashed a smile at the surprised woman. "This will look adorable on my friend here, don't you think?" The woman looked at me, muttered something in Spanish and moved.

I shook my head and held out my hands. "No way. If I think it's too short for you, it's *way* too short for me." I hated showing my legs. She dropped it on my lap anyway.

"You're brilliant."

"I am?"

She dove back into the huge pile, digging and tossing until she held up a pair of leggings, a staple of my wardrobe, no matter the season. "Here. We'll be twinkies."

"That's what I'm talking about"

Though no leggings for her could be found, the next bins did give up a long pair of gold socks and matching tops. Overall, the day at *Burnes* paid off with plenty of back-to-school treasures.

Mom seemed a little tired as I followed her down the covered sidewalk of the strip mall to find Leo. Night shifts were hard on her and when I looked at my phone, I realized bargain hunting had taken almost two hours. Mom would have to head back to work soon.

But she loved the bookstore and settled into a chair after ordering a Frappuccino. Bryn and I left her engrossed in a new paranormal romance.

Most people might think that handicapped people should be big readers, what else can we do, right? But me, not so much. The thing I love is cookbooks, so I aimed my chair straight to the cooking department. Where Bryn had a flair for clothes. I had one for food. Not that I got to cook many of the exotic dishes I found, but I loved to look.

I loved touching the shiny pictures of the big cookbooks from foreign places. There were books with authentic dishes from Ireland, France, and Scandinavia. Of course, a whole shelf was dedicated to barbecue and Mexican, but I ignored these. Although I like spicy, the grill doesn't get used much since Dad left.

The smell of soups practically wafted from the pages of *The Soup Bible*. I drooled over a particularly tasty looking recipe then snorted in disgust. I didn't recognize a single ingredient besides milk and water. *Google, here I come.*

"Hey Bryn, what's Paleo cooking?"

She looked up from the fashion magazine section parallel to my aisle and wrinkled her nose. "What are you reading now?"

I laughed and looked at the title. "*The 30 day Guide to Paleo Cooking*, of course."

"Well, I have no idea. Look at this bride maid's dress." She flashed a picture at me then buried her nose back into *The Knot*—a guide to all weddings Texas style.

It might be fun to be a chef. I winced. All that talk about the future was making me think ahead. I blanked my mind. *Nope, it's not going to work.* That's what they wanted, and I wasn't going to let their mind games get to me. They would not win this. I knew what I was. I knew no real future waited for me. All the positive, feel-good talks weren't going to change my mind.

It'd been a good day so far. I loved shopping with Bryn, but the whole inner argument I had with myself soured my mood. I couldn't imagine the foods on the pages tasting good any more, especially when I reminded myself, I would never get to taste them in the original countries. How could *I* ever travel? In no time at all, I'd put myself into a real funk.

The bright sun streaming through the huge windows, dulled. I couldn't get excited about anything anymore. Not wearing my new outfit to school, not the rented movie, nothing.

I sighed. I needed to keep the smile plastered on my face for just a few more hours, then I could go home and hide in my room and have a pity party. I turned the page to a beautiful spread on a white beach with white washed stucco buildings in the background. I looked up to ask about pancetta, and Bryn had disappeared.

I heaved *Italy Al Dente* onto the closest shelf— getting things down came easier than putting them back— and headed to find her. Usually *Allure* and *Glamour* could keep her occupied for hours. I wheeled down the end of each row until I reached the kids section at the end of the store where three toddlers fought over a huge stuffed snake.

Huh. I headed back the other way towards the middle where Mom drank her coffee. "Hey, Mom, seen Bryn?"

She didn't even look up. "Nooope."

Must be a good book.

I scanned the non-fiction and self-help section across the way. I'd never been over there, but it was either that or the gaming section where Leo hung out. Sighing, I spun my wheels towards self-help. The first sign that stuck out was a huge poster covering three aisles. Christian. Why did I know in my heart that's where I'd find her? After theology, inspirational, childbirth *eww*, and Christian fiction, I found her sitting cross legged halfway down an aisle.

She looked up and smiled with the most peaceful look I'd ever seen. Peaceful? Why did I think peaceful?

What was it about her face that made me think of quiet streams and soaring mountains? Like a landscape painting with little sheep dotting the slopes. Not a sleepy look, like Leo when he was at his best, in between snores on the couch. No. Something inside her gleamed from her eyes in a way that changed her whole face. I couldn't nail it down.

In her lap she held something as tenderly as a brand new kitten, fingers softly curled, protective even. I knew it had to be a book, but what kind of book could cause such a reaction?

I wanted to kick myself, but I asked anyway. "What'je find?"

"Look at this Bible, Tansy. Isn't it the most beautiful thing you've ever seen?"

She held it up. I had to admit. It *was* pretty, for any sort of book. Purple gemstones studded a lavender glitter cover. Silver letters proclaimed in large, religious looking script—HOLY BIBLE. I nodded and Bryn moved the book, catching the overhead lights. Reflections from bunches of tiny sequins and rhinestones danced on my shirt.

Bryn grinned. "Pretty, huh?"

Ugly words leapt to my lips. Hurtful phrases such as "kind of pretentious for a holy book, don't you think?" or "how can something that pretty be nothing but a Bible?". I bit them back. I didn't want to hurt her feelings. Especially not after just making up from a fight.

My struggle must have shown in my face, because the light and the softness that had made her already pretty face beautiful in a grown up way, disappeared and my old bestie sat on the floor in front of me again, obviously disappointed. For some reason I wanted to cry. I did that to her. I didn't know if the tears wanted to come because I had hurt her (again), or because I glimpsed something that I really wanted.

Now I knew what she meant about her knots being untied. When I gazed into her face, I think I could've seen straight into her heart and not seen a single tangle of doubt or worry. I know Bryn had troubles. Her life wasn't perfect, though sometimes I made it out to be. Being an only child, the center of her parent's whole world, created problems of their own. Her mom and dad didn't always get along. There were things that Bryn wouldn't tell even me about what went on at home. But at that instant, her troubles disappeared. Then I came along and reminded her. Here we were, her sitting on the floor, staring up at me as I tried to keep back the hurtful words.

I turned away blindly, running my castor wheels into the shelf. The whole thing teetered like it would fall. I watched it, glad for the distraction, then reached out to steady it. I hated this feeling of not knowing what to say.

Bryn was my best friend.

I could feel her sigh from clear down the aisle as she rose. "I'm just going to check out. I'll meet you at your mom."

"Okay. If you're done, I'll go look for Leo."

"Yeah, I am." She headed to the opposite wall, away from me and the long way to the checkout counter. I looked back. She had a few books in her hand, but the most obvious was the sparkly Bible.

On Sunday morning, the sky opened and a fierce rain beat down. Crushing humidity replaced the Texas heat. I stayed indoors. One, because Bryn went to church today, and two, I think I saw a red spot that might mean I'm starting to chafe. I took a shower, powdered, and stayed cool. I kept checking my phone to see if Bryn would text, sometimes she did between Sunday school and church or church and lunch. But she didn't. After church, Miz Donna was taking her daughter shopping in Longview. She always did that after my family did something with Bryn, like she was trying to one up us. I wasn't invited.

So, I was left to wheel around with nothing to do. I stayed away from my mom's end of the house; she'd collapsed from exhaustion after coming home from the hospital. Leo stayed in his room playing his video games, so just me and my thoughts bumped around the pop can of a trailer. Not fun.

I tried watching TV, but nothing interested me. So, I picked up my diary and wrote a little. That took five minutes. I stared out the window at the street when the sun cut through the clouds. It glittered for a few moments before the heat evaporated it. Pavement steamed, birds took quick baths in overflowing potholes. I wondered about the look on Bryn's face at *Hastings* and dreaded tomorrow—the first day of school.

Chapter Six

I spent the night tossing and turning. Usually, the alarm went off every two hours so I could roll and adjust myself. Don't want those pressure sores! But tonight, I just stared at the clock, waiting, rolling my legs at the appointed time, turning on my side. Making sure my hip pillow separated my knees. I think I dozed a few times, good thing the pre-set alarm kept on track. My night was not restful at all. When seven o'clock came along, I felt like I'd fallen out of my wheelchair onto concrete. Bruised, sore, my eyes gritty with sleep—broken in both body and mind.

I stared into the mirror and groaned. Great. First day of school and I looked like road kill. I hurried to the bathroom before Leo could get there and washed my face with cold water. That helped a little.

I darkened my lashes with mascara and put on my favorite hot pink lip gloss, then attacked my hair. With all my tossing and turning it stuck straight up with little knots down by the scalp. I put it in a pony tail with one of the new hair scrunchies in black and gold, and made sure my hot pink strip of hair was on top. Maybe I should change the color to gold. It wouldn't hurt to show some team spirit, even if I couldn't be a cheerleader.

When I got back to my room my phone beeped with a text from Bryn.

Bestie: Don't forget the scrunchie! :D

I smiled.

Me: Of course not! lol

Bestie: Need a ride?

Me: No. First day. Mom doing the Mom thing. :P

Bestie: Ok. Got my class list. Homeroom is 34 Mr. Reed.

Homeroom? My heart sprinted forward. My class list hadn't come in the mail last week.

"Tansy, come get some breakfast."

I shoved my school supplies in my backpack, slung it over the handles of my chair, and slid in.

I bolted out the door. "Mooom, have you seen my class list?"

Leo and Mom filled the little kitchen, so I stopped at the tiny table shoved against the window in the dining nook. "My class list." I heaved. "Have you seen it?"

Mom frowned and turned from the microwave, plopping down a thawed egg patty in front of my brother. "Nope, can't say that I have."

"It should have come in the mail last week, but I haven't seen it."

Leo tsked and squished his eggs between two toaster waffles. "Already losing stuff? You're in the big leagues now, Twerp. Got to stay on top of things."

"Oh, shut up, Leo. This is your first year in high school too."

He slathered his egg sandwich with syrup. "Well, my class list isn't missing."

"Guys, can we not have a fight the first day of school?" Mom frowned and her knuckles turned white on her coffee cup. "Maybe the list is in that pile of stuff they gave me last week at meet the teachers." She headed for the bedroom. "I'll check. Eat."

Just last year Mom rearranged the kitchen so I could reach almost everything. I snagged a bowl out of the dishwasher and poured in instant oatmeal and water. I nuked it for thirty seconds. Next, I used a thin stream of her coffee creamer to make pretty swirls. I chopped a big, red strawberry and fanned it across the top then sprinkled blueberries. A big glass of orange juice and a long drink helped clear my throat and head.

Mom dropped a paper in front of me. "Here you go. That's beautiful, Honey."

"Thanks, Mom." I wheeled over to the table to "my spot" and sniffed at Leo's mess of a breakfast.

"What? I've got everything here I need." He watched me with a gleam in his eye. *He's just jealous. He fried his taste buds years ago.* I took a big bite of my oatmeal. "Oh, by the way, cream's bad."

The putrid taste of curdled milk filled my mouth. I gagged and sputtered all over the table.

Leo leapt back. "Hey."

Mom whirled from the sink. "What's going on?"

"Why is there expired cream in the fridge?" I screamed. Milk dribbled out of my nose. I looked at the chunks mixed with oatmeal and my stomach heaved. I couldn't help it, I puked all over the table and the newly found class list.

Leo ducked out the front door. "Bye, Mom. Caleb's here."

Mom ran over with rags and towels, waving, or shooing him out the door.

"My clothes." I sobbed as I looked down at my lap, now filled with orange juice mixed with oats. My perfect first day outfit, ruined. What will Bryn say when she sees I'm not wearing the clothes we'd picked out together? I groaned. What a disaster.

Mom helped me wheel to the bathroom and while I took a shower, she ran and got me some new clothes. No way would I make it to school on time. My first tardy, already. I'm sure the teachers would be *sooo* understanding. These kinds of things were expected from someone stuck in a wheelchair. I hated it when I lived down to people's expectations.

My ponytail dripped water down my back as I hurried to the car. Wisps fought loose of the hairband and tickled my cheek as they curled in the morning heat. The clothes Mom had thrust through the door were a pair of black yoga pants and a pink shirt covered in glittery, silver butterflies. Bryn would be aghast at the fact my scrunchie totally did not match. Those types of fashion bumbles drove her nuts.

Mom pulled into the deserted drop off lane and I took a deep breath. *Here we go.* I unloaded more slowly than getting into the car. Why rush now? The bells had rung, everyone in their seats. Every eye would be on the cripple as she wheeled into class—late.

I slumped in my chair and made Mom push me up the ramp. The whole time she kept up a constant stream of words. "Remember, stay hydrated. I got special permission for you to drink whenever you need to, but make sure you make the effort to drink between every class."

I huffed. "I know, Mom."

"Oh and stay away from the stairs."

"I'm not in fourth grade anymore!" The first day back to school after my accident, I had misjudged where the ramp was and fell down the stairs. Just like the accident in the first place, she just wouldn't let it go.

"And you will leave each class five minutes early so you can get to your next class on time. Each teacher is supposed to give you any homework on a slip as you leave."

I groaned. "No, Mom."

"Don't argue. This is a big school with lots of kids and you won't make it to your classes if you are fighting through the hall."

Just another thing to make me stand out.

Mom wheeled me to the office for a copy of the class list. The one I'd thrown up on was unreadable. The clock showed nine minutes past the eight, one more minute and homeroom would be over!

"Mom, we have to hurry."

The secretary moved papers and pulled my file. *So slow.* My fingers tapped nervously on the armrest. "Here you go, Hun." I snatched the list. Mom glared at me to remember my manners.

"Thank-you." I looked at the paper. *Ms. Pereas.* My groan was covered up by the ringing of the bell and the crash of doors as the hall filled with kids headed to first class. My homeroom teacher was Coach Angel, and I'd missed the first day. I couldn't believe my luck. Even if I thought of trying out for cheerleading, which I wasn't of course, this was not the way to make an impression. Not a good one anyway.

"I've got it from here, Mom."

Mom's eyes gazed at the sea of kids moving past the window. "I don't know..."

I looked at the list. "It's okay, Math, room 45, just down the hall. I'll make it on time. Go home and get some sleep."

That seemed to decide her. She leaned down and kissed the top of my head. "Okay, if you think that you've got it."

"I do. I'm fine." She held the door for me, and I wheeled out. Like fish before a shark on *National Geographic*, the kids cleared a path. I couldn't help the triumphant smile I flashed at Mom as she headed the other way, but she didn't see.

"Tansy! Where have you been?" Bryn grasped the back of my chair and hung on for dear life. The polite break didn't seem to apply to her, and several backpacks caught at her shoulders as she tried to keep by my side.

"Hi, Bryn. Just a little hold up is all." She scrutinized my face, then her eyes widened as she took in my outfit.

"You changed!"

"Uh, avoidable, sorry."

She shrugged. "Where you headed?"

"45."

"Great, me too. At least we have one class together."

"Get behind me and push, we have two minutes left."

She jumped into position and took off.

"Hey!" Someone called as she banged a footrest on someone's ankles.

"Sorry." She sang. But there was no stopping her. The bell chimed a warning and we dashed into Mrs. Kelly's class with seconds to spare.

Despite the horrid beginning, the rest of the morning went well. By the fifth class, even *my* stomach clawed with hunger. I snacked on an energy bar as I pushed towards the cafeteria, hoping to meet Bryn. Math had been the only class we'd had together, hopefully there were more in the afternoon, but there hadn't been a lot of time to compare class lists. The back of my chair sagged heavy with books. I'd not been able to make it to my locker, even with the extra five minutes allowed by each teacher.

The first class had been difficult, especially when Mrs. Kelly nodded at me to come to the front while the class worked one last problem and she dismissed me. Leaving got easier as I barely made it to the next class. At least I had somewhere to hang my books. Poor Bryn hadn't been back to her locker yet and lugged every single one in her satchel. No wonder the news had nothing but bad to say about kids with back problems and parents complaining. Two more minutes between classes would have gone a long way to getting those books to the locker.

I pushed into the lunchroom with my castors, wincing as the door banged my leg. I didn't feel it, but that didn't mean I couldn't bleed and get a nasty sore. Bryn hurried over.

"Come sit with us."

Us?

She pushed me to a long table half filled with girls staring curiously at me. I shoved at the wisps that curled around my face, wishing I'd made a stop in the restroom.

"This is Isis, Bianca, and Sarah. This is Tansy, y'all." A blur of faces nodded at me.

"Love the pink," said a girl with a dark summer tan and black hair hanging straight down her back. Isis, I think.

"Thanks," I mumbled. I took my crumpled lunch out of my backpack and pried open an orange. Everyone was quiet. My presence often did that to people. Why did Bryn do this? At our old school we ate lunch together, just her and I. Never anyone else.

As though she sensed how everyone but her seemed uncomfortable, Bryn motioned to the group of girls. "Everyone here is trying out for the cheer squads. We're planning our individual routines." As though released from suspended animation, the girls broke into talk about tryouts. The big question seemed to be what they would be asked to do. That turned to asking and then to speculation about how to get onto the Angel Squad.

"What do you mean?" I asked.

Bryn frowned as she ticked the points on her fingers. "Each girl is supposed to have something that one, showcases her athletic ability. Two, shows team spirit. And three, shows gymnastic ability."

How did she know all that? My hands froze halfway to my mouth and wouldn't move. Why did I even care? Why ask questions? They were trying out—not me. Bryn seemed to notice my unmoving sandwich. She smiled. "I'm planning a round-off back handspring and I'm going to use that little cheer we made up."

I sputtered. *That was our chant.* We'd made it up when we were ten and each year refined it a little bit more. I tried to swallow. What was it about my food that always seemed to try and kill me lately?

While the others traded chips for Oreos®, or talked about swimming during the summer or camps, I listened with one ear, but shrank lower and lower in my chair. The peanut butter, banana, and honey sandwich tasted like sawdust. My juice, like sea water. I focused on Bryn as she used big arm gestures to talk about the tumbling she'd worked on at Bible camp.

"Bianca and Sarah go to my church," she explained to me. "We went to camp together too."

"Were they saved too?" My voice was nasty, even I could tell, and the giggly talk of the other girls died as they stared at me.

Bryn reached for my hand, her face crumpling. "Tansy–"

"Never mind. I'll see you later." I pounded my lunch bag into a little ball. I shoved away from the end of the table where I'd been parked like some sort of baggage. Unfortunately, I hadn't looked behind me, and my wheelchair didn't have that neat back up alarm like the scooters at Wally world.

"Yikes!" A crash behind me silenced the whole lunch room and every eye turned my way. I closed my eyes, counted to—well, I just took a deep breath really, the counting only worked for Mom, and looked over my shoulder. Yep, it was as bad as I thought.

Of all the people I could have knocked over, it was Jamie. He hadn't actually fallen, but his lunch made modern art all over the floor. I wanted to disappear.

"I'm so sorry." My voice sounded like a parrot squawk.

He looked from me to his lunch. "S'okay. I think they were fish something-or-others anyway." The boys behind his shoulder laughed nervously, but I grasped my wheels and got out of there as fast as I could. I tossed my bag in the trash, and once more pushed out the doors.

"Whoa there, *Chica*."

Can this day get any worse? I looked up. *Yes, it can.* "I'm sorry Ms. Pereas, umm, Coach—"

"Coach is *bueno*. Missed you in class today."

"I—was late."

"I gathered. Try to be on time tomorrow."

"Yes, Ma'am."

"You handle that chair *muy bien*. You could have taken out my knees. Stopped on a... what is the phrase?"

"Dime?"

"Yes, dime. I heard you might want to try out for my Angels." This made me look up. The heat of a blush burning at my skin. Although I have black hair it came with the skin of a cheap porcelain doll. The ones so white they look like chalk. Unfortunately, it gives away every feeling I have. Dad used to say they were running out of toner when I was made. I used to think that was funny. Trouble was, I had plenty of ink, it just came out in bursts. Like now. I had no idea what to say. She just stared at me, waiting.

My mind wandered to the strangest things. Like, who knew Coach only stood a little bit taller than me sitting in my chair? The way people talked about her in hushed tones, I thought she'd be super tall. But I nearly looked her in the eye, seated in my chair. I tried to think of something to say, but nothing came. If I told her no way, would she be insulted? Would she hold it against Bryn? I might be mad at my bestie, but not enough to get her in trouble with the coach she wanted to impress.

Coach must have realized my dilemma, or thought she did, because she stepped out of my way. "Well, hope to see you at tryouts. Brynley said you had some cool moves I should see."

Brynley? Oh, Bryn.

"Uhhh." Still nothing would come out.

"It could be interesting, for the both of us. See you in homeroom." She walked on down the hall before anything comprehensible made it out of my mouth. A tear leaked down my cheek and I brushed it away with a hard swipe.

I jammed the heels of my hands against the tires and headed in the opposite direction, mad at myself beyond words. I made it to my locker as the warning bell sounded. After two tries I thumbed the latch and threw it open.

A sparkly purple cover of the Bible Bryn loved so much stared at me. A puffy silver bow twinkled in the ugly fluorescent lights and the glimmer of lettering caught my eye. In the lower right-hand corner was my name in silver script that matched the Holy Bible title: *Tansy Fisher*.

Rage burned. Who did she think she was? She'd gone beyond cramming it down my throat—this was beating me over the head and kicking me while I lay on the floor. I grabbed the book, wanting to throw it under my tires and run it over again and again and leave it for her to find.

But it plopped in my lap as I heard her voice behind me.

"Do you like it? It matches mine. It's a b a c k -to-school present for the both of us. Mom took me to the

Christian store in Longview and I got it engraved for you."

I held the book out. "Take it back."

Bryn stepped away, palms up. "I thought you'd like it. It's perfect for us."

"Why'd you think I'd like it? It's you, not me. I don't want this book. It's nothing but lies."

Bryn looked around. Kids started to drift down the hall from the cafeteria. I think I saw her flush under her dark skin. Eyes turned and stared.

"It's not lies, Tansy. It's truth and love and strength."

"It's not for me."

"The Bible's for everyone. I thought—"

"Whatever you thought, you thought wrong." I dropped the Bible on the shiny tiles. I slammed my locker and wheeled to my next class. I couldn't bring myself to run it over.

Chapter Seven

I'd blown it. I knew that. Bryn and I had history class together and the whole time she didn't look at me.

I pulled my legs up to my chest on my bed and lay there. Teachers wanting to get a jump on the *TAKS* test had already assigned homework. But it stayed in the backpack on the wheelchair. Harsh afternoon sunlight faded to dusk through the curtains. Doors slammed as people came and left at nearby trailers. Kids, some I hadn't seen all summer as they avoided the heat, yelled and screamed in a pickup game of soccer in the street. Still, I stayed in my room.

My phone lay silent.

I fingered the keys and then typed.

Me: Sorry

I waited, and waited, but nothing came back. Maybe she forgot her phone. Maybe she was having dinner and hadn't seen the text. So, I waited some more.

Mom knocked on my door. She never knocked. I lifted my head. "What?"

She stepped into the room and I caught the bright gleam of sparkles dancing in her hand. "Bryn brought this by." She set the Bible on my bedside table and sat down next to me. Her cool fingers brushed the hair back from my head. It felt good. A tear leaked out of the corner of my eye and soaked into the pillow. For the first time I noticed the wet cover.

"Bad day?"

I sniffed. "The worst."

"As bad as this morning?"

"Worse."

She made an odd puff sound as she blew her breath out through her teeth. "That *is* bad." She reached out and took the Bible up again. It annoyed me how reverently she held it, like the leather and gem book would break. "This is beautiful. A very thoughtful gift."

"I don't want it."

I closed my eyes, wishing I could turn my face to the wall, but that would take more energy than I could muster. Instead, I buried my head in the pillow, away from her raised eyebrows.

"Why not? She even had your name engraved on it."

"She thinks I'm going to become some sort of Jesus freak like her, and I'm not." I bit my lip. "I'm an atheist."

Mom seemed surprised. I don't know why. It made no sense to me that someone like me would believe in God, or his kindness and love like Bryn had said. He was the one that put me in this chair after all.

"An atheist, huh?"

"Yeah."

"Why?"

I stared up into her face. The light streaming through my pink curtains turned her skin a pretty shade of rose—like a fairy, I wanted to touch her cheek, it looked so soft, but I didn't. I curled my hand under my pillow. "If you can't figure that out, you've got the problem, not me. Go away. I don't want to talk about it."

She sighed and stood. "I'm headed to work. See you in the morning." She waited at the door, but I didn't tell her good-bye.

I'd never realized how much I relied on Bryn to fill up my time until we weren't texting or talking or visiting. The last few days and nights had been horrid, lonely. I was bored. Leo locked himself in his room. Mom left for work.

Once again, nothing on TV. I flipped through my cookbooks, made some plans to make a fancy dinner, but after looking in the fridge, decided that wasn't going to happen. Mom really needed to go shopping, but it was rice and beans until next paycheck. I did find a package of noodles that I prepared and ate without telling Leo. *Let him fend for himself.*

I sat in front of Mom's laptop and tapped my fingers. As if on their own accord, I Googled wheelchair tricks. *Hmmm.* I watched the kid that held the world record for the most spins. *Impressive.* And here I thought I was pretty cool being able to do one. I did get a few tips, maybe shouldn't do them on the fly like I did. Better to sit and spin. I grinned at my stupid joke and moved on. *Wheelies. I can do that.* I did mini wheelies every day over little things like small curbs and power cords. I pushed away from the table. *Could I stay that way?*

I scooted my rear all the way back into the seat. *Maybe I should try on the carpet.* I moved into the living room and once again leaned back, holding my wheels tight at 12 o'clock. I kept leaning and leaning aware that the smallest shift could send me tumbling. I hated to fall. It was embarrassing. Finally, I felt my front castors lift off the ground. I hovered there for a few moments until my biceps shook with the effort. Keryn would be so proud of me. I tried again and again until I became comfortable with the sense of weightlessness. When I tried to go higher.

I hit something hard. *What's that?*

I leaned over. *Oh right, anti-tip bars.* Mom had them installed after my first few tumbles. *I'm not a baby any more. Time for these puppies to come off.*

In the laundry room, I found Mom's toolbox. It'd been a gift from Miz Donna one year after my Dad left. All pretty and pink with flowers that flaked off with use on the first broken door knob. At the time, I'd thought she'd been poking fun of us because we didn't have a man around the house to do repairs, but it'd sure come in handy.

It was heavy, but I wasn't sure what I needed, so I put it in my lap and headed back to the living room. There it was relatively easy to set the box on the couch then go from chair to couch to floor. I pulled the toolbox down and got to work on my ride.

A door creaked as I threw the first bar to the carpet. *Uh oh. Now he decides to come out of his room?* I yanked the second off as Leo shuffled to the kitchen. Right past me and the mess in the living room as though he didn't see a thing. I ignored him. Maybe he wouldn't.

"Tansy!"

I jumped as the zombie came to life with a parrot-like squawk.

"What are you doing?"

It looked bad. Me on the floor with the tools spread all around tearing my chair apart. "I'm fixing my chair. What's it look like?"

He sauntered over and leaned on the couch with a bag of chips. "Was it broke?"

Where did he find those? "For doing wheelies it was."

Whatever Leo planned to say, my answer stopped him.

His mouth snapped shut with a funny click and the room fell pleasantly quiet again. It didn't last. "Mom's gonna kill you."

I put the tools back while he watched. Getting up to the chair from the floor is a little harder than getting down. But after five years, I'm a pro. Leo didn't offer to help, but he did take the toolbox.

All the while, thoughts were spinning crazy in my head, like the anti-gravity ride at the fair. I've never been on it, but I've watched Leo plenty. The pretty lights whirling by and the people inside floating up against the walls from the centrifugal force.

Why are you doing this?

Because I want to.

You're thinking about tryouts, aren't you? Well forget it, you're a cripple

Well, that burned me up. Even though I called myself a cripple all the time, to actually hear my inner self call me that was another thing entirely.

I'm not a cripple, you are!

Okay, the argument with myself was a little weird, but there it is. I guess on top of being wheelchair bound, I'm schizophrenic.

By dark, I was doing nice wheelies and even a spin. Leo watched me like a TV the whole time. I couldn't tell if he'd fallen asleep with his eyes open or hoped I'd finally do myself in and was getting the story ready for the cops. Either way, I ignored him the best I could.

Tuesday dragged. There were good things about the morning. Such as I didn't puke all over my clothes. But Mom found the anti-tip bars where I'd half shoved them under the couch. So, of course we had to take the time for her to chew me out. Then she almost ran out of gas and had to stop to fill up, so I missed homeroom again. But Bryn never appeared. No one latched on to the hand grips and gave me push through the crowded halls. She didn't look for me and when second period rolled around, she sat in a different desk in the back with Isis and Bianca. I sat in the front where I could leave without disrupting the class.

I'd worn the black skinny jeans and yellow top we'd picked out for the first day, hoping to mollify her a little, but she never said a word. I heard my name once. I think one of the other girls asked if they should come sit by me. It was Bryn that said no.

At lunch I sat by myself near the door. Every time it swung open it almost hit my chair, but I didn't mind, it hid me from everyone coming in. Problem was, everyone that went out gave me a pitying look. Poor little invalid, sitting all alone by herself. I forced myself to eat. But it was like eating cardboard—again. Finally, I gave up and headed early to my next class. None of the teachers would challenge me, after all, I left class early.

Mom dropped me off in the clinic foyer for PT. "I need to run go get some groceries. You okay?"

"Of course." She waved and hurried away while I headed towards that creepy cartoon hallway. It was gone.

I stopped at the top of the hall that led to the PT doors and checked around to see if I was in the right spot. Everything had been painted white. Stark, painful, pristine white. I wheeled slowly towards the double doors with the little glass inserts. No one rushed in or out. I tried to peer through the paint, to see that bunny dripping blood, but could make out nothing through the whitewash.

Sometimes music greeted me as I came to PT. The volume undulating as nurses, parents, therapists, moved in and out through the doors. Today, nothing. The hall seemed to narrow, constricting down until I felt like Alice in Wonderland growing larger. No way I would I fit through that rabbit hole of a door at the end by the time I got there. I also knew that whatever was on the other side, I didn't want to see.

I misjudged the weight of the door and flung it open so hard it crashed against the stops. The sound reverberated down the deserted hall. But no one yelled at me. I wheeled in. A funeral home pall hung over the silent exercise equipment. I shivered at the analogy—*bad choice Tansy.*

"Hey," I called.

Movement in the corner caught my eye. I almost turned around to get out of there. The feeling was just too creepy. But it was Keryn and Heath sitting on the weight benches. They seemed surprised by my presence.

I frowned. "What's going on?" It's not like I hadn't been coming here forever on Tuesdays. "Where is everyone?"

Keryn leapt to her feet. "What are you doing here? I thought administration called everyone."

Mom had probably been sleeping and not heard the phone. "For what?"

Keryn's eyes cut to Heath and then to one of the glassed-in offices on the far side of the room. That's when I noticed Tye, Meg's PT. He sat with his feet up on a desk, staring at a corner. I stared too, trying to see what drew his attention. A huge spider (one of those yellow and black kind you see outside mostly), had spun a great big web. It shook the web gently, as though sensing the PT's presence, though he sat absolutely still.

No other clinic worker appeared. Looking at the

clock confirmed what I suspected. *Yep, late.* About right for me recently. Two days into school and I couldn't keep up with my schedule.

Keryn put a hand on my shoulder. It was ice cold, not her usual warmth. And she didn't smile. Something was up. I wish they'd just spit it out already.

"We canceled PT today."

I blinked in surprise, not expecting that one. The only time I'd known my sessions to be canceled were because of ice storms and when the air conditioners pooped out. It was plenty cool in here, and just a few minutes ago it had been 900 or so degrees outside with no ice in the forecast. "Why?" I started to dig for my phone, but Keryn's stillness stopped me.

"Meg's in the hospital."

My stomach clenched like I'd just fallen out of my chair, but instead of landing I just kept falling. Instantly it all made sense. The missing nightmare animals, the skeleton crew, the whispers, the looks. I'd seen this before, though I tried to block it out. There were other things that shut down this wing of the medical center. Death was one of them. I'd been coming here five years. One of the longest—of the children anyway.

Right after I'd started coming one of the PT's had been killed in a car accident. I remembered the funeral home quiet from back then. Taking a closer look at Keryn's face, I noticed the red-rimmed eyes, mouth a hard, flat line despite her effort to smile and reassure me. It wasn't working. I didn't have to ask. I knew this was no accident.

I'd seen it coming. Meg retreating into her music, snapping at Tye. Everyone had known something bugged her. It'd been too much to handle and she'd tried to end it. Fingers clasped my phone too tight, the numbers beeped angrily. I glanced down. I wanted my Mom.

Keryn squeezed my shoulder and I shook her off, trying to dial. My fingers refused to obey. I dropped it in my lap and shoved my chair away from her grasping hands.

"Tansy—"

The rage boiled. "Why?" I screamed "Why didn't you do something? That's your job isn't it? Why didn't you tell her about the music and thinking about the future instead of me? Work on her brain for a while, huh? You just let her go." I remembered Meg slamming out of PT last Friday, the look on her face. I'd thought she was so strong. I'd been wrong. Everyone had been wrong. She'd been on the edge of shattering.

I paid no attention to the hands that reached for my phone. Nor to Keryn calling Mom to come back in a hushed voice. The rage inside me froze slowly to ice until I was numb all the way through, like my mouth after a Popsicle®. My heartbeat slowed, then stopped. My lungs squeezed tight, pushing all the air out and then refused to fill again.

I wanted to reach out, but the ice kept me from moving. It kept me from crying. The words "shock", and "let her rest and work through this" and "schedule a visit to her counselor" flowed over my head like water under a frozen stream. But it made no difference. There was nothing left inside to hurt.

Chapter Eight

My alarm sounded way too early Wednesday. At first, I thought it another rollover alarm, so I picked my legs up and started to get adjusted. Where most people toss and turn through the night, I don't. Just like how I have to be careful during the day not to sit in one spot too long, the same with nights. It takes some getting used to, but I always have to be on alert for those pesky pressure sores.

Then I read the clock and groaned. Time to get up. For just a moment it was a normal day in the life of a para.

Then everything from yesterday flooded back.

I rolled over to get a good look at the saying I'd tacked on the wall. What if I didn't have any music left in me? What if there were no strings left to make it on? Is that how Meg felt? Empty? Frozen? I shook myself. *I didn't have the answers.*

I pulled myself into my chair and started digging through my dresser for clothes. I hadn't laid them out. What was the point? The absence of Bryn took the fun out of planning what to wear so I went with black stretchy skinny jeans again, because hey, I can wear them without a problem with sticks for legs. A black top. It fit my mood.

This afternoon Bryn would go to cheerleader tryouts. A pain grabbed at my chest and I wanted to cry. Our friendship hovered on the edge of a cliff, it may have already fallen off. After yesterday, where she ignored me all day and her not answering my texts, now she would become a cheerleader with new friends and a busy schedule of practices and games that didn't include me. She'd step into that future that Keryn kept hounding me about.

And what would happen to me? Would I wind up like Meg? She must have felt abandoned by everyone, even the boyfriend that put her in the chair, to do what she did. Now, that terrible loneliness stalked me.

I banged my fist on my chair. It wasn't fair. Bryn still had all her strings. She could make any sort of music she wanted. She could be Beethoven or Lindsey Sterling. She could go anywhere.

The room shrank as that anger inside me curled and

smoked. Was it possible for someone to spontaneously combust with rage?

At that moment, Leo decided to stick his big head with his slicked down hair through my door. "Mom says to get up."

I threw the nearest thing at his face—my diary. "Will you knock, already? I'm up!"

He didn't go. His eyes slid to the paper stuck on the wall. "You know that saying's not true, right?"

What?

"It's just an internet story. I checked it out on *Snopes*."

The fire in my chest boiled up and over. I rammed the foot plates into his shins.

"Hey! Cut it out!"

"Are you happy now? Why do you always gotta be so negative? I hate that! I hate YOU! Get out! Get out! Get out!" I grabbed the handle and slammed the door in his face, hoping I knocked all his teeth out. At the very least broke his nose. People like him drove people like me over the edge at high speed.

I didn't feel any better on this side of the door. The thin plywood cracked against the wall as I slung it open again and chased him down the hall.

He gaped at me, dabbing at the blood that trickled from his nose. "What's wrong with you?" He howled.

"What do you mean 'What's wrong with me'? You're the one that came snooping into my room-got to read my stuff." Each word I punctuated with a threatening jerk of my chair. "You stay out of there, ya hear me?"

Leo backed quickly, trying to protect his shins with his free hand. "Get off me! Mom! She's totally lost it."

Mom's worried face appeared at the end of the hall. "Why must you two start EVERY SINGLE MORNING off with a fight? It's only the third day of school." She had to scream over the racket of me yelling.

I paused and took a deep breath. Leo leaped in first. "I'm just trying to explain that stupid saying she's always mooning over is a hoax. I thought she'd want to know."

"You didn't. You're just being mean." I jerked the hand grips again. I felt compelled to defend Keryn. Even if the story wasn't true, I knew she was trying to get me to think. "It doesn't matter anyway, does it? It's the point of the story. Maybe if Meg had known about the music, she'd wouldn't have slit her wrists." I covered my mouth. Tears squirted.

Mom stepped between us as Leo dove onto the couch.

It didn't stop his mouth, though. "It's sad that people need to rely on made up stories about real people."

I nearly ran over Mom in my frenzy to get at him. He hadn't heard a word I said. *Meg almost died.* "You're missing the whole point, idiot."

"Follower."

"Jerk."

"Stop it." Mom roared in a voice I'm sure rattled the

skirting four trailers away. "Stop it now."

My ears rang with the sudden silence.

Leo shrugged and turned away. "Whatever."

I made a face behind his back. "Just stay out of my room and stay out of my stuff."

Mom shook a warning finger at me. "Enough, I said." She sighed and turned back to the kitchen. "Oatmeal?"

"I don't care." So cold cereal is what I got. Plopped it in front of my spot with a force that made the milk jump and sugar encrusted flakes scatter. She tossed Leo a wet paper towel for his nose then stood at the sink and stared out the pollen decorated window until Leo left for school with a grunt.

Mom turned to me and I hunched in my chair. *Oh boy, here comes the talk.*

"What was that all about?"

"Nothing."

"Awful loud for a lot of nothing."

I slammed down my spoon. "I hate how he snoops in my room. He had no right."

"I know. I'll talk to him about it. You did give him a bloody nose, though. Maybe he *was* trying to help. What was it?"

"It's a story Keryn told me, about a violinist, Isthek Perlman. He broke a string and played a whole symphony straight through. It's supposed to be a famous saying about making music with what you have left."

Mom looked out the window as she thought. "I like it."

"Yeah, I did too. Keryn kept ramming it down my throat enough. She should have given the talk to Meg though, she's the one who needed it. Of course, if she has an older brother like Nosey, I'm surprised she didn't try it before."

Mom's raised eyebrow spoke volumes, and I stopped my tirade. But she surprised me by changing the subject. "Are you catching a ride with Bryn today or do you need me to take you?"

I looked into my cereal. "Can you? We got into a fight." It was selfish to ask, she needed her sleep.

"Tansy."

I know, it looked bad. Seemed like I'd picked fights with everyone lately. "She just won't lay off!"

"Seems like you've been saying that a lot lately."

"So? I swear everyone's out to get me. Like there's this big conspiracy. Keryn wants me to think on the future. Bryn wants me to become a Jesus freak. Then Meg goes and..."

"And you? What do you want? Do you think Meg's way is the answer?"

"That's just the problem, Mom. I don't know." How could I explain this to her? "It's like I'm all twisted up inside. Everyone pushing me just makes it worse."

Mom turned back to the window. I studied her profile. She was so beautiful, even in her scrubs with dark brown hair pulled tight in a messy bun. But she looked so tired...and sad. Guilt bit me. I knew the fights with Leo didn't help. He started just about all of them, though.

"The answer is in the still small voice."

"What?"

"It's in the Bible."

"Really?" I had no idea Mom knew the Bible. We'd not been to church since Dad left. All I had were dim memories of funeral-type songs and old ladies hugging me.

"Elijah was a prophet. Queen Jezebel wanted to kill him, so he had to run for his life."

I knew the name Jezebel and that everyone thought she sat at the tippy top of wickedness, but I'd never known why. "So, what happened?"

"Well, the Lord told him to stand on the mountain and wait and He would come. See, Elijah had been filling God's ear with complaints about his life. He'd done everything the Lord said and the thanks he got was that people were trying to kill him."

"Sounds like a good reason to complain to me."

"So, Elijah went out and waited. First came a hurricane that shattered the rocks. But it wasn't God. Then came an earthquake and a fire."

"Let me guess—still no God." *Just like Him not to show up when needed.*

"Nope. Last came a gentle whisper, and there was the Lord. That's when Elijah found the answers he needed."

"Cool." I sat for a moment and realized that was the longest speech I had heard come out of my mom in a long time. She didn't seem to talk much anymore. It amazed me even more that she knew that whole story out of the Bible. "How'd you know all that?"

She stared off again, uninterested in answering.

She glanced at the microwave, her coffee cup clattered into the sink. "We've got to get. We'll be pushing not to be late."

I hated to rush from the table right away. Mom's story had quieted the anger. The knots loosened just a bit. I imagined that if I stayed right there, if nothing changed, I could feel like this forever. Peaceful? Maybe not like Bryn's. But with just Mom and me—maybe one day. Something nudged inside me. My frozen heart beat once, twice.

"Can I stay home, Mom?"

She froze, her hands buried in my backpack. Her eyes searched my face with that soul-eater gaze. I wanted to turn away. But I let her look. Only the third day of school and I wanted to skip out.

I could see her weighing everything in her mind. Did I need time alone? Was Meg's suicide attempt affecting me that deeply? Even I didn't know the answers. Maybe if I stayed still that whisper would come, that the Lord would give *me* the answers. Then the moment ended. Mom's searching face hardened though her hand was soft as it pushed back my pink stripe.

"I think you need to stick this one out, Tansy. Be with your friends. Maybe even talk to Bryn about Meg."

I dropped my eyes away from her face. Bryn and her Jesus.

She grabbed the push handles and out the door we rushed. As we left, I realized today was tryouts. The peaceful feeling stayed in the house.

Chapter Nine

Bryn avoided me all day again, and by the looks her new friends gave me, she'd told them everything. *Christians! Yeah right.* Bryn was the only person I'd ever met that I even considered an example of what Jesus would want to see. Even now when she wanted to throw me under a bus.

Somewhere between math and lunch, I made a decision. I planned to be a better friend. I'd go to tryouts and I'd support her. I'd hoot and holler the loudest. I'd scream until they kicked me out.

In Texas history, I smiled at her as I took my seat at the front. She stayed in back, but her eyes seemed sad. I dug in my pack to cover my hurt. But what did I expect?

I'd thrown her beliefs, her gift, in her face. Who'd want a friend like me anyway? Always so nasty and up in her face. Had I only liked Bryn before because she was so easy going? Let me have my own way, even before my accident? If so, that was changing today. She'd see.

I got to leave Integrated Computer Applications 15 minutes early. I hurried to the gym without stopping at my locker. What was the point? I carried all my books in a second bag hanging off my chair anyway. I think I'd opened that locker two times since the beginning of school.

A sign fluttered limply in the air conditioning when I got there.

CHEER TRYOUTS

MOVED TO THURSDAY

4:00 SHARP

Really? The little bit of nerve that had carried me through the day and even down the hall to the doors of the gym, fled. Like a balloon with all the air gone, I deflated. Flat, abandoned, lonely. The sign might explain why the hall was deserted. Of course, Bryn and the others would have heard the announcement in homeroom. A class I'd missed again. I thought of the after-school detention I would be serving on Friday and fumed. Someone could have told me. But why would they? I'm the cripple after all.

The sound of a basketball made me pause my inner rant. Who was in there? Someone else who didn't get the memo? I tried to peek through the glass, but my ride only brought my nose to the bottom of the door's glass. If someone had come in from the other side, they might not have seen the note. I'd better check. I'd hate to be left by myself while everyone else went about their business—like now.

I eased open the door and tried to see around it, but the basket and the player were at the other end. Neither in my eye line. I sighed and pushed all the way in.

A lone player shot from the three-point line. *Swish.* All net. He retrieved the ball and shot again, this time from the side. *Swoosh.* Watching him was fun. He never missed a shot, the ball seemed to run back to him every time. He jumped. The flow of his arm arced, the ball rolled right off his fingers and into the net again. I didn't recognize the player. He was older, but not any teacher that I knew. The door slammed behind me and the guy turned. That's when I saw he was missing an arm.

"Hey," he called.

I stayed where I was. "Hey."

He strolled towards me, ball bouncing. I didn't know if I should get out of there. All the stranger danger training from elementary beat at my brain. My hands gripped the push rims, just in case. "Sorry. I thought that maybe someone didn't see the sign."

"S'okay. I'm here to let people know who didn't get the memo."

I should have thought of that.

"Oh, okay."

"So, who are you?"

Perhaps his injury triggered the introduction I used in PT. "My name is Tansy. I'm a T10 incomplete."

He blinked, pausing half a second, that awkward silence that told me I'd said something weird. "That's not who you are—that's your medical condition. I could say I'm a transhumeral or AE amputee—but I don't." No one had ever said that to me before. It made me wonder. If I wasn't my medical condition? What was I? Who am I?

"So, what are *you* then?"

He grinned as though waiting for the breakthrough in my brain that would lead to that question. He turned, flexing the stump of his arm. There a tattoo of an eagle grasped a snake in its beak and a globe in its talons— behind an anchor on its side. Shadowing it all was a large Celtic cross. I studied the intricate art for a moment, admiring reds and blues. I'd never seen the like. "I'm a soldier of the one true King." Pride dripped from his voice. Kind of tacky for a grown man to say, like he invested too much into role playing games.

I had to ask. "What do you mean?"

"I was the only one in my unit with a cross on my arm and near my heart." He held up a silver chain with a cross made of nails. "I was the only one that survived the insurgent attack that took my arm." I'd never met a soldier before, maybe he suffered from PSTD. My skepticism must have showed, because he laughed again and started bouncing the ball. "Now, I travel around and give talks to church groups and stuff."

"What about?"

"God."

I frowned, seemed like everyone couldn't wait to jump on the religious wagon. "That's nice."

He paused the bouncing. "Yeah, it is."

Questions started to pop up in my thoughts, and just like that, they burst out of my mouth. "How can you still be a Christian? After God let you lose your arm, I mean?"

"Actually, losing my arm might have been the best thing that could have happened."

My mouth gaped open like a fish. "Really?"

"Sure. It opened my eyes. I thought I was a strong Christian, but all the pain, surgeries, everything I went through, actually drove me closer to Christ until finally I understood He was the only one who helped me keep my sanity." His face turned far away, like he was in another country. "So many didn't make it. Even if they lived. They got angry. Destructive." I thought of Meg. I knew how that went. His shoulders shook. "But you don't want to hear about all that. Sometimes I help out my mom too. Like now. My cousin had an emergency with her baby, so here I am—telling people Cheer tryouts are tomorrow."

"Wait. Your *Mom* is Coach Angel?"

"Sebastian Pereas, at your service." He touched a finger to an imaginary hat, cleared his throat and stood soldier straight. "So, since I have been assigned this important task, it is my duty to inform you. Come back *mañana.*"

Heat flared in my cheeks. "Why would you think I'm here for tryouts?"

Sebastian tossed the ball towards the basket even though he stood well past the half court line. *Swish.* "Because this is where tryouts are. Aren't you a cheerleader?"

I gaped. Maybe he'd been shot in the head too. He seemed a little odd. Couldn't he *see* me? "But I'm in a wheelchair."

He trotted off to retrieve the ball but stopped and looked up as though I'd said the stupidest thing in the world. "So?"

"I can't walk. How could I be a cheerleader?"

He stared.

Uh oh! Here is comes. Another super deep lecture. What's with everyone lately?

But he didn't. Just shot another basket. "Yeah, I can't walk either. Just don't tell anyone."

Is he making fun of me? "That's not funny. I see you walking."

He shrugged and pulled his basketball shorts up to show me his thigh. I nearly puked. Most spinal injuries don't leave many scars. In fact, paras appear pretty normal. But this guy's legs looked like someone tried to make meatloaf out of them while still attached. A waffle scar ran across both thighs and down past his knees. Smaller scars crisscrossed down his shins, disappearing into his socks.

"Bomb just about blew my legs clear off. Doctors didn't think I'd be able to use them. I'm here today because of *Dios* and the prayers of *mi mamá*. Do you have a church, Tansy?"

I looked at his shiny black sneakers. "Uh, no." *Could he ask me that at school?*

"Well, First Baptist is having a back-to-school bash. You should come. There'll be food, games, music."

Again, another perfect shot. Who was this guy? The door opened on the other side of the gym and Coach Angel bustled in.

"Sebastian! Didn't you give Tansy my message?"

"I knew it."

"What, *Mijo*?"

He grinned at me over his mother's shoulder. "That she's a cheerleader."

She rolled her eyes at him and then smiled at me. "Of course, she is, or planning to try out anyway."

I ducked my head. "I'm just looking for Bryn."

"*Bueno.* But you come back tomorrow, *entiendes*? I want to see these moves Brynley tells me about."

I got out of there as fast as I could.

Chapter Ten

I wheeled down the pokey hall and knocked at the door to my brother's lair.

"What?"

I tried the knob. Locked. "Hey, will you take me down the street to the church?"

A bed creaked and a narrow crack appeared. A dark eye peered through the opening. "What?"

"Will you take me to Bryn's church?" He frowned and started to close the door. A nudge inside me told me I needed to convince him to go.

"Coach Angel's son said there's gonna be a back-to-school bash tonight. There'll be games and food and stuff."

The door opened wider. "Food?"

If anything could perk my brother's interest, it was the promise of some sort of meal. "Yeah. That's what he said."

Leo glanced back into his room. The light from his desk illuminated a rumpled bed where a book and papers lay scattered. He shrugged. "Okay."

Got him.

The parking lot overflowed with everything from jacked up trucks to small sedans. Leo puffed up the driveway. His breath blew hot in my ear, but I didn't complain. Sweat dribbled like rain. That grossed me out, but that last hill might as well be Mount Everest. No way could I make it on my own.

Leo looked around. "I don't see anyone."

"With all these cars someone's here." I pointed to where music seemed to float from behind the church. "Let's try over there."

Leo walked off. "Push yourself. I'm done."

"Thanks a lot."

"I got you up the hill, didn't I?"

Rounding the brick corner of the massive church took longer than I expected, but the music got louder, so I knew I was headed right. "Whoa!"

Behind the last corner was a stretching lawn transformed into a fair. Booths and bounce houses and a stage with long purple curtains sprung up like flowers. A live band played background music while bunches of kids chased between adults.

Leo perked up as he spied several friends. "Xander! Gage!" He waved and took off without a backward look. I didn't mind. He started to reek like boy. *Ewww.*

I pushed forward, my tires sunk into the thick Bermuda lawn, so I swerved and kept to the sidewalk that meandered through the booths towards the stage.

I'd had no idea all this space was back here. A few years ago, the First Baptist Church bought up several empty lots and built this humongous church. Bryn and her mom started right away—been going ever since.

Most of the kids swerved wide when they realized the chair and I were permanently attached. Adults I didn't know, smiled in a sad way, like they knew my pain. Teens avoided me. I didn't see anyone I knew. At least, not anyone to talk to.

I wheeled down to an area set up on a sloping hill with a stage at the bottom. A few lines of plastic folding chairs were occupied, but most people had brought their own. I smiled. I had too, but my insides told me I didn't belong with these Jesus freaks. I didn't belong anywhere. I settled into a spot to wait for the main event.

The band picked up the beat and people gravitated

towards it as though connected by a string. A woman came on stage and began to sing.

A deep-throated alto rose high over the shrieks and talking. At first, I didn't get every word, then it seemed the world came into focus around the song.

Over the crowd, our eyes met. *"What if you're right?"* she sang.

Right about what?

More questions poured from her lips, questions I asked myself whenever Bryn started going on about Jesus.

Goose bumps prickled up my arms despite the infernal heat, making the sweat run down my back. The lyrics changed to a different question.

"But what if you're wrong?"

A couple in front of me raised their hands, fingers pointed to the sky. Some girls my age-linked arms and sang along. They knew every word.

The question plaguing me was this: what if all these Jesus freaks *were* right? They seemed happy, swaying to the music, eyes closed, drinking in the beautiful music and haunting words. An old man to my left nodded solemnly with the beat. More people gathered. What was it about her? She wasn't beautiful, passably pretty. Not fashionable or dancing around like a stage production on TV. Her simple skirt and sun top were kind of plain. The singer didn't leave time to wonder about it, the song changed as though she talked directly to me.

"You're running away...His plan may catch you by surprise."

She had to be talking about Jesus. The knots in my stomach twisted and jerked, tightening into a ball. I gagged. Quickly, I swallowed and fumbled for my backpack. *Where's that bottled water?* At last, the cheap plastic crinkled under my fingers. I took a deep swig. The lukewarm liquid helped me get control of my nausea. Rage pushed back.

I wish she'd end it already and get to the main attraction.

People dropped what they were doing, left kids in the hands of frantic teens, pressing closer to the stage. Many of them were young girls, eyes riveted on the woman. But the more people that approached, the angrier I got. Sure, I was glad the stage sat at the bottom of a slope so that I could see the singer even from the back. She stopped and swayed as the pianist and guitarist jammed out with sweet music that tickled me to my toes. My legs jumped spastically, and I pushed them down, glancing around to see if anyone noticed.

Only a redheaded kid watched. She stood facing backwards, attached to an adult by a harness that looked like a dog-walking contraption. Three-years-old maybe? But her eyes weren't focused on my jerking legs. She stared at somewhere above my head. Self-conscious, I put a hand to my hair. *Was it sticking out?*

"Pretty."

I melted with relief. She obviously meant my pink stripe. I smiled. She picked her nose. All happy thoughts disappeared. *Gross.*

The distraction helped me control my runaway feelings. The music stopped, the singer headed off the stage. She hugged someone coming on. I narrowed my eyes, trying to guess what was next.

Surprise washed over me. Sebastian! He walked on the stage like he owned it, waving and grinning. He said he'd be here, not that he'd speak to the crowd.

"Hey there, y'all." Girls sighed and clutched their chests dramatically, obviously at his Texican accent. *They've got it bad. Yeesh.*

He hadn't dressed up like *I* thought someone should to give a talk at a church. His dress code seemed to be tank tops and shorts. The waffle scar stood out pink against his dark skin. I looked around to see what people might think about him showing off the injuries. No one seemed to pay any mind.

A couple of teens heckled good-naturedly from the front row. "Hurry up, Pastor Seb."

Pastor?

He looked up. "Just let me get this mic adjusted. I want y'all to hear this, feel me?"

The crowd clapped and some shouted "amen brother". He seemed to be a favorite with everyone, particularly the kids around my age.

"Are you ready to hear *The Word*?" he asked suddenly. His sharp eyes peered over the crowd. He pointed here and there. More yells. Then he looked straight at me. For a second, I heard or saw nothing but him. He broke the spell with a smile and a wink. Heat rushed to my cheeks. I jerked my chin down as the sounds of the fair came roaring back.

"Good. 'Cause I'm here today to let you know an important truth you gotta hear." He paused. "Jesus has got you."

Got me? What did he mean?

He looked straight at me and said. "You just can't do it all by yourself."

I gulped and looked around. What was it with the people on stage talking to me?

"I'm telling you, *niños y niñas*, you can't do it. That hole you're trying to fill up with smoke and dope, rage, friends, whatever—it's not going to work. You don't got the strength. Oh, you might think you can..." He said more, but I'd heard enough. He'd read my mind, knew what I thought and felt. Goose bumps pricked again, this time I could have sworn I could feel them on my legs.

People all around nodded. I gulped. I knew the weight he talked about. It rested on my shoulders like a VW Beetle—an old one made of metal. And that hole inside? Mine overflowed with knots and anger. It wasn't enough. I knew it and it hurt. I slumped in my chair.

"But it's not hopeless. Jesus holds the world in His hands and He has a plan for you. He will give you the strength you need to throw off those chains dragging you down. You're an instrument, but right now you're broken." He chicken-walked across the stage, his neck jutting out like he had a grasshopper stuck in his throat. The crowd breathed and laughed a little. "But not without Jesus, *chicos*, not without Him. God made a promise. He sealed with His blood." He held up a book with a hard-used cover. "Now get out your *Biblias*."

A few groans came from the up-close front section.

Sebastian waggled a finger at them. "Surprise. You thought this was a back-to-school bash, didn't you? But you know me, get 'um out. Go ahead. No one's laughing at you for bringing it."

As though with a mind of its own, my hand reached in my backpack once more. My fingers collided with the Bible Bryn had given me, all hard and soft at once. Why had I shoved it in? I don't know. But I had.

"Okay then, open to Philippians 4:13."

Hey, that sounded familiar. Hadn't Bryn given me those numbers before? My fingers itched for my phone, but Sebastian moved on. Pages rustled in the sudden silence, punctuated only by the youngest kids still enjoying the bounce houses. My fingers fumbled, the Bible dropped on my lap. What was I doing? I had no idea how to find whatever he said in this book. It was huge—the type too small. I started to shove it back into the pack. Soft, brown hands stopped me. I looked up into Bryn's face.

She smiled. "Need some help?"

Did I? Without waiting, she flipped open the sparkly cover and thumbed through the pages. Jealousy pricked me. She made it look so easy.

"Here it is." She pointed at a number at the beginning of a paragraph. Sebastian watched the crowd, waiting until the page turning grew quieter. I looked around. All eyes were focused on the stage. Waiting.

When he read from the Bible it seemed like his microphone got jacked into a 100,000-watt megaphone. His voice reverberated through the crowd. "'I can do all things through Christ who strengthens me.'" How did he know that God could put me back together? He didn't even know what was broken inside me?

Through his whole speech, I felt a tugging, a ripping inside. Something clawed to get out—or in.

But Pastor Seb didn't wait for me to figure out the mess in my head. He just kept right on pounding away at me with his words. "Okay, Peeps, give me something you struggle with, you don't think is in this book."

For a moment, no one answered his challenge, then a voice piped up. "Anger."

"Too easy—Paul."

"Not enough anger."

"Quit playing with me—Timothy. Give me something harder. Something you struggle with."

A tiny voice piped up from down in front. "Abuse."

Other voices rose, shouting out problems both big and small. How did they find the nerve to bare their souls to everyone? But their problems were hidden, they had to be shouted out for anyone to help them, right? My problem, those stupid, crippled legs, sat right out for everyone to see. But another issue beat at my brain, one not particularly mine—but could be.

"Suicide!" *Oops, did I say that?* Heads turned my way. Yep, that was my big mouth. Thoughts of Meg lurked in the back of my brain, even if I refused to see them. Sebastian never missed a beat.

"Elijah."

Isn't that the man Mom told me about?

"The point is, everyone in the Bible had problems. They didn't let those problems get in the way of trusting God. Even when they did, God used them anyway. Like Samson and Jonah. I was in the middle of a war I didn't understand when *boom!*" He pointed to his scars. "I was broken. Not just here." He thumped his chest. "But here."

"M*i mamá*, she prayed, and God answered. He put me back together again. You may look at me and think 'Dude, you're missing an arm'. I say, 'yeah, you're right, but I'm whole on the inside. Come on, *amigas*." He pointed at me.

"Claim the promise He made to you. God wants you back. He wants to make you whole."

I snapped my Bible shut. That's it. Proof of a conspiracy. Somehow, everyone had this all choreographed. That thing that clawed at me? No way would I let it in.

It's just not fair. How did they all know to gang up on me? How did Sebastian know exactly what to talk about? Maybe he was in cahoots with Keryn? Okay. So, it might be a little selfish to think that everything revolved around me, but proof seemed everywhere.

The beat started again, the musicians pushed Sebastian off the stage with hugs, back slaps, and a drum roll. *Wow, everyone likes him. Yikes. Is he headed my way?*

He might be, but hands reached out, stopping him. Kids gathered around, clamoring for attention. I turned my chair to escape and ran into Bryn.

"Isn't he great?" She stared dreamy eyed at Sebastian. "He's our new youth pastor."

"Yeah, I met him."

Her eyes sharpened on me with interest. "You did?"

I nodded, not wanting to talk about the empty gym. "Hey. I'm not feeling so great. I think I'd better head out." That distracted her from whatever she planned to say next.

So much better at being a friend than I was. She was great that way. I bowed my head at the little lie.

"Do you need some help? I could get Mom. We can

drive you home."

"Nah, it's cooler now." The sun played peek-a-boo behind the trees, teasing the sweaty participants of the rally with the prospect of dusk. Lights around the perimeter clicked on with loud buzzes competing with the cicadas in the pecans. "I'll just find Leo." Another lie. I needed to get out of there, preferably before Sebastian got up the hill. Besides, if I stayed and listened to any more music, any more talk, that thing beating at my heart might make it in. I hugged the darkness and anger closer. *Mine.*

"Oh, okay. See ya at school?"

I forced a smile, positive I looked sick enough to be convincing. "Sure."

"Try not to be late again—It's only the fourth day."

I tossed her a fake glare over my shoulder. "I know. I'm set for some sort of record. How many times can I miss homeroom?"

Sebastian broke free of the crowd. His eyes met mine. "Tansy!"

I slapped my hands on my tires and got out of there, pretending I couldn't hear him. Cripples can do that. People expect that just because your legs don't work, the rest of you doesn't work either. That wouldn't wash with Sebastian. He'd been where I was. But for some reason I couldn't face him.

My wheels hit concrete and I flew down the path. People had thinned out some, most gathered around the stage to listen to the talk and music. A few mothers hovered around the bounce houses for those die-hard kids who didn't mind the suffocating, rubber scented heat. Most got out of my way fast when they saw a hot pink wheelchair barreling towards them at high speed.

Leo sat with a few of his buddies at a ball toss game. Is *he handing out candy? They're getting him too.* I shook my head at him and headed for the parking lot.

Chapter Eleven

I didn't feel like going home. Even thinking about putting myself back into the metal can of a trailer felt suffocating. As though it was too small for all the great big thoughts running around in my heart. I could see the skirting, the missing piece grinning at me like a kid with a missing tooth. I shuddered. Better to face the mosquitoes than that empty, mocking shell of a home.

The vicious sun finally relented and dipped behind the trees, giving the gasping earth a brief respite from the heat till dawn. Still warm enough to make sweat trickle in ticklish places. Fickle puffs of wind brushed my face with blistering promise kisses that never amounted to much.

I turned my chair towards the park. The thought crossed my mind that Mom wouldn't be too happy with me wandering around by myself, but when was the last time she'd called to check on me? I had a phone, didn't I?

The basketball courts and the park lay deserted, except for one die hard skater looping back and forth in the tube. He never pushed it to the top—the rails most likely too hot to touch. Didn't he know about the back-to-school bash just down the street? People getting saved and all. The music from the open stage thumped on the heavy air, but a music of a different sort whined above it. The skipping melody floated from the hill covered in headstones like daisies. I coasted past the chain link fence encircling the cemetery, trying to find its source.

Edwards Cemetery claimed a small rise at the north end of the park. The monuments once white, now had the look of speckled turkey eggs. The plots rose in tiers with retaining walls at odd, though I'm sure perfectly reasonable, positions. Several walkways meandered through a variety of headstones—short, tall, old, new. Squares set aside with paving bricks outlined plots, some fenced with trees growing thick around the rusted iron corners—some lay empty of everything but grass.

Is this where Meg would have been buried if she'd managed to kill herself like she wanted? I tried to find a stone to fit her personality, but that was too morbid, even for my dark thoughts.

The odd thing about the winding paths was that they started and stopped without any warning. As though a family paid for a few feet of concrete, but the relatives of the next dead guy didn't want to, so the walkway stopped. One path had a bench in the middle. Like once upon a time it served as the end of a path, then oops, someone got a little money and added to it.

One of my favorite things to do, though it's kind of a creepy habit, is to read the inscriptions. Bryn and I tried to calculate the age of the dead person and speculated about how they died. I especially like those with pictures. The names never seemed to match the face, especially the odd ones like Ollie or Hitch. And why were the pictures always of young people when the dates showed he died in his nineties?

Tonight, a simple melody danced from the tree shrouded section reserved for children. The one with the tiny headstones and names like Infant Smith or Son of JH and DL Hall. I didn't go there much, but tonight I headed towards the sounds.

The sky turned more gray than pink, so I turned my wheels faster to investigate before dark and the sound freaked me out so much I chickened out and beat it for home. The notes sang a strange tune, high and whiny with a giggle thrown in. It's how I imagined a burbling brook sounded. When I read that phrase in a book I always think, what does that sound like? Why can't they describe it better? There's not a lot of moving water in Texas, least, I've never seen it. We have tanks. Large ponds the color of dried blood where cows stand to cool off.

Finally, I glimpsed a figure wavering in the heat waves let off by the forest of tiny headstones. Still too early for ghosts, so I ventured closer. My ears tuned themselves to the music. How beautiful! It lilted through the air like the voice of the woman I'd heard earlier. The melody both happy and sad. My feet wanted to dance to the lilting melody (if they could have) The melancholy whine brought tears to my eyes at the same time. The notes could have been the music the wind makes in the oaks before a storm. The sound of rain crashing into a thirsty earth during an unexpected shower in the dead of summer.

I craned my neck to see who could make music that moved me like that. An old, black man perched on a folding stool in the shade of a tall pine. A bow flew over the strings of a scratched-up violin. Pink palms flashed as long fingers pressed the strings on the neck. I knew without asking he played to the grave at his feet. He stopped when he saw me.

"'Ello there, Missy."

I nodded and came a little closer. The violin fascinated me, especially after the Isthek Perlman story. It amazed me that such music could come out of the little instrument he cradled against his cheek like a kitten. "Hi."

"Lil' hot to be out, don't cha think?" His voice scratched, like he had a cold, and he swallowed the ends of his words.

It took me a moment to figure out what he said. "You're out here."

"So's I am. Toda's Yvie's birthda', and she so did love a goo' son'."

"It's sad." That sounded rude, so I added. "And happy."

"Shue it is. But that's how I feel when I think of my baby, all happy and sad."

I studied the stone at the end of his leather, work boots. Yvie Black. 1940-1953. I swallowed at the dry knot in my throat. Thirteen. Like me. A homemade shrine in the shape of an A-frame dollhouse crouched over the tiny stone. Pictures, unrecognizable ink blots faded by sun and rain, perched on the little shelves. Toys, figurines, and flowers adorned roof niches. A teddy bear leaned beside the stone. Obviously, a birthday present.

The old man plucked a string, then another. Like rain on the roof of the trailer they thrummed an answering chord in my heart.

"You can keep playing, if you want."

He looked at me a long moment, his eyes black holes rimmed in white. He took a kerchief out of his overalls and wiped his violin, then his face. Setting the instrument under his chin, he drew the bow gently. The battered instrument leapt to life in the same happy/sad song. A celebration and a dirge in one.

I closed my eyes and let it wash over me. "How'd she...?" How do you finish such a question?

He pulled a long note and stopped. "She fell."

My eyes popped open. Dark had fallen with the suddenness the long Texas dusk misled you to expect. Streetlights now illuminated the night. Uneasiness crept over me. She'd been thirteen and died from a fall?

"She must have fallen a long way."

The notes shivered across the cemetery. "No. Off'en a horse."

"Ouch."

"Texas was different back then, all hard and slow. She was ridin' to town like a'ways. A truck popped off and down she come."

His head bobbed over the violin again, but his eyes lingered on my ride just a little too long. "Neva made it to a chair like yourn, jus' lay in bed and wasted away. On her thirteenth birthday, she went to be with Jesus. I's happy that she was finally at rest, sad because she had so much livin' left to do. Leastways, that's what I thought. God knows what He's doin' though. Next summer typhus too' away her sisters. She no could have stood it. She loved those gals." He swiped at his eyes with the kerchief. The violin sat silent. Two more stones caught my eye. Little lambs sleeping on top with matching A frames. Suzie

Black. Annie Black. The sisters. "Jus' proved to me, no matter what the devil's gonna heap on us, God's got something bigger in mind. My babies' angels now. It were a great comfort to their mama and me."

The heat disappeared as a chill skittered down my spine, spreading to my fingers. Thoughts of me, and Meg, the accident, and Jesus all mixed up in my brain. "I gotta get home." But my voice bounced off the stones. The black man blended in with the dark shadow of the tree. I blinked, trying to focus. But he sat still, as though he'd disappeared.

The lights of the basketball court beckoned me, beacons of hope to the sudden fear that clutched at my chest. A couple of streetlights lined the perimeter of the cemetery, but none reached to the interior. I turned my chair and wheeled down the path, bumping slowly at first, then faster as the feeling of being watched tickled my shoulder blades. The mixed-up jumble of half-forgotten memories of my own fall chased me. Blood throbbed in my head in time with the pounding of my heart.

Headstones loomed on every side. Mocking my questions but giving no answers. Tears blurred the lights.

My chair tipped hard to the left. Falling. My fingers clawed at the opposite armrest. I had to right myself. Too late. I'd come too close to a retaining wall in the dark. Nothing stopped me from going over.

An armrest thumped into my ribs. My breath

whooshed out. I lay stunned, half out of my chair, hair sticking to grass already dew damp. *Breathe, just breathe.* I ordered my collapsed lungs. With a shrill wheeze, they obeyed.

The concrete wall loomed above me and then the night sky. Stars twisted in a dizzying dance. *This is actually kind of nice. I've not looked at the sky in a long time.* I should be getting my phone. I should call for help. But I didn't, not right away anyway.

I don't know how long I lay there. It could have been a few minutes, maybe an hour. Mostly my mind just blanked, but every once in a while, I thought on how the black man had disappeared and I knew in my heart that I'd seen an angel.

I argued with myself a little. It could have been a ghost or a demon, but his message was the same that others, like Bryn and Seb, had been telling me. That God had a plan. And then he'd disappeared. All this thinking made me uncomfortable, so I paid more attention to what was going on around me and getting out of this mess I'd put myself in.

My skin itched and thoughts of fire ants and chiggers took precedence over deeper things and got me looking around for my pack. *Just great.* It'd been thrown clear. My phone chimed teasingly and a side pocket lit up then went black. *A wonderful time to run out of battery, Tansy.*

Grabbing a fistful of manicured grass, I sat up and reached down to untangle my legs. My elbow throbbed, ribs ached. What kind of beating had my legs taken? My heart jumped into overdrive as thoughts of scrapes and cuts turning infected took over. I resisted the urge to rip my leggings off and examine the skin. *Deep breath, deep breath.* What good would it do to strip down to my underwear in the park when I couldn't even see? Who knew what could crawl into my—okay, not thinking about that.

Why is it so dark? Swiveling my head, I realized the court lights were gone. Had they been turned off? Was it that late? Reaching out in the dark, my fingers brushed stone. I'd fallen between two retaining walls—a hole. I couldn't see out, and no one could see me. Fear brushed my gut.

To get my mind off morbid thoughts of never being found (until the grass needed mowed sometime around September), I studied the tipped wheelchair. I needed to get it up. I inched closer, scooted my shoulder under the armrest, and pushed. It rose a few inches and stopped. I didn't have the leverage of a lower half to push it higher. If I got on the other side, I could pull on a tire. I walked on my hands to the wall, my legs dragging behind. But the tires were too close to the wall to get my body wedged between. I tried to push the chair away. It dug into the lawn.

I slammed my fist on the ground. "Stupid chair!"

I looked back to the night sky, so wide and spreading over me. The God who made that seemed so far away. Did He even know about me? If He did, why did He allow my life to be such a mess? I stretched my hand up and blocked out a few of the stars. Wouldn't hurt to try, would it? "God? If you can hear me. I really need a little help right now."

"Tansy. Tansy." Voices called my name over and over. *Wow, that was fast.*

I pulled myself towards the opening. "Here I am."

There were searchers at the skate park.

I cleared my throat and called again. "Help."

Bryn's voice called out. "I heard something."

"Me too. Over by the cemetery." Pastor Seb. They were looking for me.

Hope made my voice louder. "Over here. Help."

Two shadows leapt into view, a flashlight running, then Bryn knelt by my side. "Tansy. What happened?"

"I fell."

The light beam ran up my legs like a scanner off a sci-fi movie. Sebastian brushed at clinging grass. "Anything broken?"

The light seared my eyeballs. "Acck! I don't think so."

Bryn leaned closer. "Ouch. You're bleeding."

I licked my lip and tasted blood.

Pastor Seb flipped my chair upright with a smooth foot and hand combo and pushed it closer. He leaned down. "Put your arm around my neck and hold on tight." His stump pushed into my back as his whole arm snaked under my knees. I flew upward and landed gently in my chair.

Bryn shook her finger in my face. "What were you doing out here, Tansy? You told me you were going home! That you'd get Leo."

"I changed my mind."

Sebastian started my chair forward, the castors dug into the grass and we came to a stop. He grunted as the push handles jabbed him in the gut. My tire thumped. Bryn got out of my face and moved to the back of the chair. "I think you bent your wheel."

I groaned. "Ugg. School's tomorrow."

Bryn thumped me on the shoulder. "You had the whole neighborhood out looking for you and all you can think about is school?"

I dropped my head, glad they couldn't see me blushing in the dark. "The whole neighborhood?"

Bryn giggled. "That's hardcore, Tansy."

Seb cleared his throat. "Hardcore or not. We need to let people know you're okay. Why didn't you answer your phone? Bryn called every few minutes."

"Oh, my pack." Seb went back for it while Bryn pushed me out to a walkway. Hopefully one that didn't end at a retaining wall. The chair jerked as he thumped it on the armrest. He let Bryn push me while he made a phone call. The first went to my mom.

"We found her. She's okay. Just beat up a bit." Mom's voice screamed over the phone and I cringed. Boy, was I going to get it. Had she come home from work?

"How did you know I was missing?"

Bryn voice tickled my ears as she puffed up the drive out of the park. "Leo came up to me at the festival looking for you. When I said you'd gone home, he went there."

Seb snapped his phone shut and then dialed another number. "Hello, Mrs. Winters. We found her. We're taking her home. No, I don't think she needs to go to the hospital, but we'll look her over when we get her home. Thanks for your help." Phone snapped shut again. "Hey, *Mami*. Found her..."

Yeash, they really did have the whole neighborhood looking.

"Leo came back just as we were getting everyone together to clean up. He was freaking out that he couldn't find you anywhere." Bryn sighed. "I wish I had a big brother."

I remembered bashing his nose in with the door. "No, you don't."

"Anyway, we teamed up and started looking. Adults went with the kids to help." She leaned down and gave me a shoulder hug. "I'm glad we're the ones that found you."

I nodded. "Me too." Fighting back tears. I owed them an explanation. "There was this old man, he was playing the violin and I wanted to see. Then it got dark and he disappeared, and I got freaked so I hurried faster, I fell."

Ahead a car zipped into the trailer park. Mom.

Seb tucked his phone in a back pocket then patted my arm. "It's okay, Tansy, you're safe now. But you do have to face the music for worrying everyone."

As we neared the trailer, the left tire thumping, I spied Mr. Santi in his lawn chair. He jerked a flashlight at my face and for the second time that night my eyeballs got seared.

"*Nina*! You are safe!"

I gaped at him. "I didn't know you spoke English." They weren't kidding about the whole neighborhood, even the guy who never left his porch was doing his part.

He smiled, flashing gold capped teeth in the porch light. "Of course, I do. I'm glad you're home." He stood and turned into the trailer. But the time we reached the top of the ramp, the lights in his trailer had gone dark.

The door flung back with a bang and Mom stood framed by the flaming light. "There you are!"

I gulped. *Oh boy.*

Chapter Twelve

Funny how fast that marine and my best friend beat a retreat at the anger in Mom's face. But I didn't blame them. Her hands jerked through the air as she laid into me. Leo leaned against the hall door, nodding, and frowning in agreement with each wave, but ready to dive into his room if her wrath turned on him. Which it did after a while.

She jabbed a finger at him. "You! What were you thinking? Losing your sister like that?"

"But, Mom. She took off."

"Doesn't matter. You get to your room. I'll deal with you later." His face got bug-eyed and he disappeared.

I felt bad for all the trouble I'd put everyone through.

I didn't mean it. But there were things I wondered. So, as she ranted, I tuned out. Her hands pointed and waved in anger. I remembered how she'd held the Bible, how she'd been able to tell me a story I'd no clue existed.

"Mom?"

She stopped her mid-pace and whirled on me, hand raised. "What?"

I crouched back and braced myself. But she didn't strike. I cleared my throat. "Have you ever prayed?"

"What?"

"I mean, for me, when I hurt my back? Did you ever ask God to help me?" Wow, I've never seen my mom lose her anger so fast. One minute I was positive she meant to hit me, the next she dropped onto the couch and covered her face. Her rasping breath filled the small space. Was she crying? Not my mom. She was too strong.

Blood pounded in my ears as all the bumps and bruises began to make themselves felt. She glanced up as I licked the old blood where I'd bit my lip.

She leaped up, grabbing a rag from the sink. "Strip," she ordered. "Let's see how bad this is. Sebastian said a three-foot wall. What were you doing? Trying to fly?"

I dropped my eyes. She avoided my question very neatly. Not looking at me, she jerked my shirt over my head. I hissed as she took an alcohol-soaked cotton ball to the patchwork of scrapes on my arms. Finished, she pointed at my pants. "Leggings off." I glanced towards

Leo's room. I hated anyone seeing my legs, but no way would he venture out until ordered. She leveled a hard look at me. "Now!"

I shimmied out of my leggings. Dark Dallisgrass seeds tumbled to the linoleum, a sand burr pricked my palm. Mom sped up the process by grabbing the hems and jerking. Long fingers poked at the dark blue bruises forming.

"Well, did you?"

"What kind of question is that? Of course, we did."

"We?"

She glanced up. "Your Dad and I. We prayed like crazy."

Really? I tried to imagine my parents posed in a picturesque hospital scene from a Hallmark movie. It didn't work. "So why didn't He answer your prayers?"

Mom went still for a long time. I tried to twist around to see her, but her hands forced my cheek away as she continued the torture with that blasted disinfectant. "Owww."

"Hold still."

"Are you going to answer me?"

"He did answer our prayers. You're alive, Tansy."

I snorted. "Half alive."

With the fingers grasping my chin, she forced my face back to look at her. "Don't say stupid things like that.

You're very much alive. You can do anything you want and you're not laying in some coma somewhere or in a cemetery."

I jerked my face away. "So, if your prayers came true, and we were one big happy family, why did God put me in a wheelchair and make Dad leave? Doesn't seem like that was any way to answer someone's prayers."

Mom sighed and knelt in front of me. "He didn't leave because of you, Tansy."

"Oh yeah, why did he leave then?"

Mom stared away. It struck me again how quiet she'd become. I remembered a different mother. One that laughed and made cookies. My mouth watered at the dim memory of a kitchen filled with the smell of cinnamon. What I wouldn't give for one of her Snickerdoodles. She'd changed since the accident.

I'd ruined everything. Rage fissured through me, coiling and tightening knots up my arms and down to my stomach. Maybe I should have died. Mom and Dad would still be together. Maybe she'd still smile and talk.

Dangerous thoughts fluttered, shadows of dark things best left undisturbed. Is that how Meg felt? That the world would better off without her? Are these the thoughts that led her to try and die?

I gripped my armrest in sudden understanding. A cold sweat broke out as goosebumps chased up and down my arms. I didn't want to understand her. I didn't want to be like her. But it was so easy to see how that path would open to someone like me. A few little cuts and I could put right every wrong my accident caused.

Mom shook herself. Perhaps she sensed the darkness pressing in around the small trailer. "Dad didn't leave because of you, Sweetie. He left because of me—my anger. I'm the one that couldn't handle a kid in a wheelchair, not him."

I pushed my chair back. No way, not my mom. She'd been so strong. Every little dirty deed required, she'd done on her own. She'd changed my diapers for goodness sake! She'd rearranged the house, gotten a job. Made sure I still went to PT when most kids dropped it after a few months.

I jabbed a finger at her, like she was the kid, not me. "You're lying. You're doing that thing they do in the movies to try to make me feel better about Dad leaving, right? Take it all on yourself so I don't hate him? Right?"

She shook her head and stood. "No, Tansy. My anger pushed him out—not you. He needed to get away from me or it might have destroyed him as well. Don't ever think it was you, Sweetie." She leaned down and gave me an awkward hug. "But we're alright now, right?"

Her voice begged me to agree, her tears shimmered like clouds full of rain just waiting to burst. The bones of her shoulder pressed into my forehead. She needed me to say yes. I could only nod.

Her breath whooshed in my ear. "Go get your shower. School tomorrow."

After my shower, I tried to organize for the next day. My shoulders screamed with each push of the wheels and opening drawers, turned into a production. The overhead light illuminated spectacular bruises blooming like Black-eyed Susans up and down my legs. I dragged myself onto the bed but couldn't sleep.

For a long time, I lay like a vegetable and stared at the wall where Keryn's saying had hung, just thinking of nothing—and everything.

In just two days I'd met two men who'd every reason to hate God, just as much as me I suppose—but they didn't. They'd found something good in all the tragedy, linked by the belief that God had a plan for them beyond what they could see. Despite everything—my hate, my anger, my tantrums—did He have a plan for me too?

I shook my head. What would He do with me? I'm just some dumb teen who'd broken her back. Why bother? I'm not some great person on course to change the world—just a crippled teenager in a middlin' sized Texas town.

Pastor Seb's words bounced back at me—those about getting fixed and making music that could make a difference. I held my breath. Had I ruined some great cosmic plan by not believing in Him and looking for the good? Had I become so focused on the things that I couldn't do that my eyes were blinded to those I could?

Hard to think that insignificant, crippled me could be a part of something great. I definitely didn't want to end up like Meg. But how did one go about getting in with God? It was clear to me that I wanted more of that positive thinking that Bryn, Pastor Seb, and even that old man that might have been an angel, displayed. I didn't want to end up in some bathtub filled with blood *eww* and miss the chance to do something awesome. Could I really ask Him to show me how to be a part of His plan?

My fingers fumbled for the Bible I'd placed on the night stand. I flipped the pages. The answers were here—somewhere. I tried to find the verse Pastor Seb had read tonight, but I couldn't, so I turned at random. Nothing jumped out. The words didn't make sense. Frustrated, I snapped it shut.

My head thumped against the headboard and I almost texted Bryn, but as my eyes drifted closed, a picture appeared in my head of praying as a little girl. When was that? I don't really remember church, but it must have been from that time. I knew then that I needed to pray, to actually talk to Him about what I wanted—no needed.

I folded my hands. "Lord, I don't feel like I should be a part of Your great plan. I've been mean and nasty to everyone—and I'm really sorry about that. But I don't want to be like Meg. If you give 'em, I want a second chance. Please help me make the music that you want me too"

Did it sound corny? Sure, it did. But the moment I opened my eyes, a sense of relief flooded me. Like all the things that had tied me up inside didn't matter. If I could just let go and trust God to take care of things—He would. I thought of all the people He'd put in my path lately, Bryn, Seb, and the old man. That conspiracy I thought was going on? I knew now it wasn't Mom's—but God's. His love surrounded me. He'd tried so hard to get my attention, I'd just been a little dense is all. I hoped now I could do more of what he wanted me to do with my life. That reminded me of school the next day.

Before I lost my nerve, I folded my hands again. "And God, if you don't mind. I'd really like to be a cheerleader."

I waited for the anxiety that would have me almost puking with fright as I thought about tryouts—but it didn't come. Instead, I felt like I'd been at a sleepover with Bryn and I'd had too much sugar and not enough sleep—all giggly and light. Like I could do anything and everything. Climb Mount Everest, be a four star chef, anything at all. It felt like I drank the most potent energy drink ever.

My legs jumped like they were going to try out for cheer on their own. My eyes popped open and the gritty feeling that told me I'd hit tired and should sleep was gone. I stared at my chair. "You're gonna get fixed, you worthless hunk of metal."

Swinging my legs over to my chair and then to the floor closest to the thumping tire was easy. I gave the whole thing a shove and watched with a smile as it tipped and fell—against my desk. "Darn."

I inched closer and spun the tire, trying to see the problem. I couldn't see anything. It didn't look bent, but it definitely shouldn't hit every rotation.

"What's going on in here?" Leo demanded from the door.

The tire flashed in the overhead light. "Knock." I said, because that's what I always did.

He ignored me—like always—and stumbled the rest of the way in, fisting his eyes. "It's one in the morning, Tansy. What are you doing?"

"My ride's broke and I want to try out for cheer tomorrow." I gave it a shove. "I can't figure it out. Does it look bent to you?"

"You're trying out?"

I concentrated on the tire. I didn't want to see the look I knew was on his face—the one that declared me the stupidest sister in the world in his face. "Yeah." I wanted to tell him about my talk with God, but it still felt new, embarrassing really. So, I didn't.

It surprised me when he plopped down beside me and gave the tire another push. "You're trying out in this?"

If he hadn't been half asleep, I would have hit him.

"Duh."

"Why?"

Now I looked at him. He must be sleep walking. Did he mean, why would I use the only ride I had, or why would I try out at all? I played it safe. "Because I can." Then, because he *is* my big brother, I asked, "Is it stupid? To try out, I mean?"

He surprised me again with his answer. "Nah. But what changed from the other day when you couldn't do anything?"

I glared at him. How did he know that? He just twisted the chair this way and that, his eyes half closed. His hair all dark and curly like he was five.

I sighed. "It's time to get off my butt and try something, don't cha think?"

He shrugged. "Sure." Leaning forward, he plucked something out from the back of the wheel. "Here you go. You had a pecan shoved up in there."

"Really, that's it?"

He tossed the green covered nut to me. "Yep." A cold knot started in my stomach. No excuse now not to do what I was bragging about. Then a strange thing happened. Almost as soon as it started, I thought of God and His big plan, of making the music I should, and it was gone. Leo eyed me as if trying to read my thoughts.

A smile burst out of me and I reached over to hug him. "You're my favorite brother, you know that?"

He patted me at the same time he pulled away, like I was a pit bull—friendly now, but liable to attack at any moment. "I'll remind you that the next time you try to break my nose."

I shrugged. "You deserved that—"

"Did not."

"Anyway, you're supposed to say, 'I'm your only brother'. But I'll try to remember both the next time you don't knock." I balled up one fist and mock threatened him but grinned at the same time.

Finally, he lost that wary look and smiled back. "Nothing holding you back now, you've got tryouts in the bag."

"Thanks."

He heaved himself up and stumbled out of my room with a little wave. I pulled the chair closer, locked the brakes, and used it to hoist myself into bed. So much for staying up until morning. I was beat.

Chapter Thirteen

I didn't wake up when the next two rollover alarms went off. Instead, I palmed the reset button, moved my legs over, and flopped back to the pillow. So, of course, it didn't register when the wake-up alarm went off—they all sound the same after all.

The door slammed against my wall mirror as Mom burst into my room. "Tansy. Why aren't you up?"

"What?" The morning sun slanted through the pink curtains as they blew in the thundering air conditioner. It definitely didn't seem bright enough out there for morning.

Mom spoke slowly. "It's eight o'clock. Get. Up. Now."

"Eight o'clock? I should be at school." Cheer tryouts were today and the coach my homeroom teacher. Once again, the day started off on the wrong foot. I struggled to focus. Hadn't I just closed my eyes?

"My point exactly. Leo's been gone for an hour."

Jerk left me sleeping like a baby while he headed for a perfect attendance award. I reached for my chair. My elbow screamed with agony. I turned it over. A big, purple bruise flashed like a streetlight, complete with grass stains I'd missed in my shower. Throwing the covers back, I examined my legs.

At least I'd been wearing the usual leggings last night. They'd protected my bony legs from a lot of the scrapes I might have gotten. But black and blue bloomed everywhere. I didn't have a lot of muscle or fat for protection. I sighed, knowing Mom watched every little move, trying to gauge if I could make it to school or not.

How easy it would be to throw myself on the pillows and beg off. I *had* taken a beating after all. Maybe that's not the best way to start off a new life in a great big plan.

I looked up and tried to smile in what I hoped was a reassuring way. "Not so bad, huh?"

She came closer and ran knowledgeable hands down my legs, lifting them up like she might be looking for a vein. I felt nothing where she touched me, but my heart beat hard each time she paused. If she decided I shouldn't go to school, I couldn't try out. What then? There weren't make ups, even for cripples—not that any had tried out before that I knew of.

"You're in pretty rough shape, Tansy."

"I know, Mom, but it's okay." She looked at me kind of weird, as though trying to figure out why I wanted to go so bad after trying to shirk the other day. I opened my eyes wide and inched towards the chair. "I'm just a little sore is all. I just need to loosen up." I bit my lip. Should I tell her? "I'm trying out for cheer today. If I don't get to school, I can't."

She stood up, dark brown eyes hard and searching. Then her breath whooshed out. "Okay then, let's get going."

I headed for the bathroom at lightning speed.

"No time for a shower," she called after me, disappearing down the hall. Good thing I'd taken one in the middle of the night.

As I rolled up the ramp to school, I tried not to moan. Even my hands felt raw, despite the gloves to protect them. My biceps screamed, but I dared not complain. I didn't let a whimper cross my lips, not with Mom watching me like a hawk. She turned into the office to get me a permission slip for missing homeroom—again—and I let out the breath that I'd been holding.

I watched a few kids meander around the glassed-in library, ignoring the eyes of the office secretary watching me. Her displeasure at issuing another late pass radiated into the hall. *No kidding, Lady, I'm disappointed with myself.* I didn't need other people getting on me to make it worse. I hoped Coach Angel would give me a chance to get my stuff together.

Mom held out the slip that would get me into my second hour class. "Detention Friday."

"Again?" I burst out. She frowned. *Oops. Did I forget to mention that one?*

"What do you mean, again?"

"Umm, I was late Monday," I ticked the days off on my fingers. "—and Tuesday, and Wednesday. The last one, Ms. Pereas gave me a detention for missing homeroom." Should I mention this was only the fourth day of school?

Mom stared at me for a long minute, then she crouched down to look me in the eye. "I'm sorry, Tansy. It's been kinda crazy, hasn't it?"

I shrugged and looked away. "Yeah, but it's not your fault."

She nodded. I couldn't tell if it was in agreement or if she was talking to herself. "We'll get it figured out."

"Do you mind me trying out for cheer?" I should have asked her before, but it burst out now. I wanted her to want it like I did.

"I don't mind at all. What's a little more crazy, right?"

I nodded. "I might not even make it."

"I bet you will. You just keep up the good attitude and shine. But even if you don't, it's that you tried. I like that."

I wheeled close sideways and hugged her. "Thanks, Mom." Wow, after a famine of hugs seems like our family was doing it all the time now. I'd even hugged Leo. Mom seemed surprised, paused, then leaned down and wrapped her arms around me so tight, my head threatened to pop off.

"I'm proud of you, cheer team or not. I just love that you're going for your dreams again."

"Will you pray for me?"

She drew back but kept her face close. "I'm a little rusty, but of course I will. When are they?"

"Four o'clock."

"I'll set my alarm."

I gave her a little arm hug. A couple of the kids in the library peered through the glass at me. I felt like a goldfish even though they were the ones in the bowl. "I'd better get going—before I miss another class."

She gave me a push. "Go on, get outta here, Kid."

I wheeled towards room 54, knowing I had yet another person on my team. I felt stronger, things felt easier. Things like wheeling into class late and every eye turning toward me as I interrupted Miss Radford's lecture was easier. Meeting Bryn's eyes and knowing I had something important to tell her was simple and exciting, and the thought of trying out for cheer, well, it just seemed like something I should do. No more doubts, my bestie had been right all along—wouldn't she love to hear that. Even thinking of the apology I owed her, about everything, didn't seem so daunting, and I would do it all. The determination to be a better friend still stuck, even if she always ended up being the better girl between the two of us.

Language Arts and science dragged until lunch. I couldn't focus and when Mr. Pritcher asked me what the difference between mass and volume were. I couldn't answer. Nothing from the previous three days registered at all. Thanks to my not paying attention, the class got a pop quiz. That did not go over well with my classmates.

When I pushed into the cafeteria, however, I stopped. Where to go? Do I take position by the door again, the lonely cripple? Do I find Bryn? Would she even sit with me?

I scanned the room, a few eyes turned to meet mine, but most dropped right away, and heads ducked. No one wanted to be the one to invite me over. At first, I wanted to throw my lunch at them, show that I didn't care what they thought.

Then I found Bryn's eyes watching me. They were framed by new black and gold glasses that matched that new plaid skirt, long gold socks, and white blouse we'd found at *Burnes*. She smiled wide when she saw me dressed in our twin outfit.

"Twinkie!" She cheered across the cafeteria. Every doubt disappeared. With my bestie is where I belonged. I pushed my chair towards the group huddled around the table. I didn't get a good look at the others, but I assumed they were the same that she'd been hanging out with. Bryn rushed to meet me.

She fingered the matching headband I'd thrown on at the last minute. "You wore it. And matched everything besides."

I stuck my tongue out. "Of course, I did." *Yeash, her faith in my ability to dress myself is zilch.* "It's tryouts today. Gotta have spirit, you know."

If I thought her smile was big before, it became blinding now. "Get over here. We'll plan while we eat. Everyone else has to change into workout clothes, but you—" she looked down at my ever-present leggings, "you just get to take off your skirt, lucky duck."

The other girls slid their lunches down as I took up the spot at the end of the table. I took a good look around. The last time I sat here, I'd nearly killed Jamie. He sat several tables away, nose buried in a book while his brother and a gang of rowdy boys joked around him. As though he felt my gaze, he looked up and made a mock grab for his tray. I wrinkled my nose at him, then smiled and turned back to the girls. Bryn hadn't missed the little byplay and nudged my shoulder, but the others hadn't seen. *Good. I don't need them teasing me about him on top of everything else.*

Bianca and Sarah leaned in close, eyes riveted on Isis. Curious, I tuned into the conversation.

Conscious of being the center of attention, Isis flipped her long black hair over her shoulder and cleared her throat. "Okay, this is how I hear it'll go down."

"How do you know the info's good?" I didn't want to be catty, but I also didn't want to put my trust in outdated information when so much was on the line. My immediate future hung in the balance. I needed to know everything I could. I was playing catch-up after all.

Isis sniffed and motioned everyone closer. This worked for others, but not the cripple stuck at the end of the table. Bianca looked at me, then took hold of Sarah arm, Bryn grabbed Isis, and the conversation continued closer to my end of the table. I looked with thanks at the petite Mexican. She flashed a smile back then turned back to Isis.

"I heard this from an eighth grader who's on the game squad. She is trying to make the Angels this year."

Four sets of eyes turned towards me to see if this would work. I nodded okay, that sounded like a good source. Isis once again became the center of attention. Warmth flooded me. The beginning of a sense of belonging with these girls began in my gut. They didn't seem shy around me anymore, they weren't even surprised at my question.

"First, we'll be divided into groups, then we'll start doing routines to see how well we can follow. Then comes the tough stuff. They start dividing us up into different squads by ability." I leaned in closer with everyone else, hanging on her every word. Finally, a glimpse into how this would go down. "She said they'll change a lot, but one will get smaller. If you're on that one, it's the Angels. The finale is the individual routines. Rita says it gets pretty intense as the girls try to outdo each other."

"How do you know if you're cut?" asked Bianca

"They announce that at the end, everyone that's cut comes out of the big group. They're asked to leave, then practice starts."

Individual routines? How could I have forgotten? I'm gonna have to wing it. Besides all that, how would I be able to keep up with a squad of girls? I can't dance, jump, clap when I'm moving. I reached for that bigness inside me that had taken the place of all the knots and filled the void. I closed my eyes and tried to let go of the worry. Instantly a soft reassurance filled me. Coach Angel had told me to come. God had made it clear I should go. He'd had Leo fix my chair, hadn't He?

Chapter Fourteen

I rolled my shoulders, testing my muscles, then bit back a groan.

Bryn gave me a worried frown. "You okay?"

I nodded. "Just a little tight from my flying stunt last night."

Bianca smiled at me. "I'm glad you're okay. Everyone got worried when you couldn't be found."

I bit my lip. Should I tell them what I thought? I dove in before I could second guess myself. "I think I saw an angel last night."

Instantly, everyone's attention laser-beamed on me.

Isis snorted. "What?"

"I went to the cemetery because I heard this strange music. When I got there, there was this old man. He told me about his daughter that died when she was thirteen. She fell off a horse."

Bryn raised her brows at me, the only one of the group that knew the significance of that story.

"Then it got dark, so I took off and I couldn't see the walls." I shrugged. "So, I fell."

Sarah broke her silence. "So why do you think it was an angel?" Obviously, *she* was getting into the story.

"Because he disappeared."

Isis rolled her eyes. "Yeah, right."

I glared at her but continued for the others. Who cared if she believed? "I looked towards the lights, when I looked back, *poof,* he was gone. At first, I thought he blended in with the tree, but I don't think so. I think he was an angel."

"An angel in the cemetery?" asked Isis. "At least it wasn't a ghost." She flicked her wrist, all attitude, but I ignored her. No one else seemed to doubt.

"So *why* see an angel?" asked Bianca. "You think you gonna die?"

I shook my head. "Nope. I think it was to convince me I needed to live." Everyone stared at me, obviously not understanding. But they didn't know about Meg, or all the things that had been going on with me. They just knew me as the para who couldn't get to homeroom to save her life and had screaming fights with her best friend in the hall. I turned to Bryn, pleading with her silently to understand without forcing me to go into all the gory details in front of all. I wanted her to forgive me for being such a jerk. This probably wasn't the best place, but only her opinion mattered. "I am going to try out for cheer."

The others seemed shocked. Like maybe Bryn hadn't told them about me and our dreams. It felt good to know that I hadn't been replaced as the person she told everything to. I should have known. That just wasn't like her to talk about our secrets.

Isis leaned back from the snugly group we'd made. "*You're* trying out?" She glanced at Bryn. "I thought you were just, you know, cheering on your friend."

My bestie straightened and leveled a glare at her new friend. "Of course, *she's* trying out. She's got some great moves." I hid a smile, thinking about those sit and spins I'd been practicing. She'd like those.

Isis looked me up and down. Even though the table hid a lot of me, I could feel her eyes burn a hole through the hard plastic and strip the leggings from my skinny legs. "I don't get it, how?"

Bryn grinned her shark smile. "Just wait and see. Coach Angel already knows she's coming. Said she's looking forward to seeing what she can do."

"Reeaally," Isis drawled.

Bianca balanced on her hands, putting her body

between me and Isis, obviously torn between supporting Isis or me. "Let's just see, right? It doesn't hurt for anyone to try out."

Sarah nodded. "Coach Angel knows what she's doing. She'll make the best decision for the Angels and cut who needs to be cut."

Isis came back towards the group. She fit like a missing piece of the puzzle, but her eyes narrowed at me. "We'll just see what we'll see."

I nodded back. "I guess we will."

My shoulder blades itched, like someone watched me. I looked left and right. Jamie ducked away when I met his eyes, but the hand curled around his book gave me a thumbs up. I smiled, hoping he could feel it, and hope that no one saw me.

I glanced at Bryn. Her eyes sparkled. *Ahh man, caught again.*

For some reason the things that should have bugged me, or would have just yesterday, didn't anymore. Like it was okay to look at a boy I thought kind of cute. All kinds of roads lay open ahead of me. I could be a chef and a cheerleader, and maybe one day—have a boyfriend.

I looked at the little group gathered around me, then at Bryn. For sure she would make the team, she had all the right moves. On top of that, she had rubber bands for joints and could nail a back handspring in her sleep. One more step and she'd be doing back flips.

I didn't know if the things I could do would fit in with what Coach Angel had in mind, but the thought of not making it didn't seem to hurt so bad. Oh, it scared me alright, but not so much that I wouldn't go and try for it. It felt good to know that Someone else had control of this mess down here, that Someone bigger than me with a master plan. It took away so much of that worry about things I couldn't change anyway.

Inspiration hit. "Hey. We need to have a party—after tryouts."

Isis leaned in close, her eyes crinkled at the corners as she smiled. "What do you mean?"

A party girl after my own heart. Maybe we'd get along after all. "In a few hours, maybe some or none of us will make the team. I think we should get together after to—I don't know, celebrate those that made it, and encourage those that don't for next year."

Bianca sat back, nodding. "I likey."

"Me too." Sarah chimed in.

I didn't miss that slanted look that went around the circle as each girl eyed the others as competition for a few coveted spots. No one knew how many slots had opened up during summer break.

Under the table, I crossed my fingers. Hoping that at least two spots were for me and Bryn. How much fun would cheer be if I made it, and she didn't? Or vice versa? At that point, I didn't think about the others, Bryn mattered most. I worried my lip with my teeth. If only one made it, well, I hoped my bestie got it.

In Texas History, Bryn plopped beside me, clutching her stomach. "I don't think I can do this."

"I'm glad it's not just me freakin' out."

"I got butterflies so big, I went to the bathroom and dry heaved for five minutes.

"Ewww. TMI." I studied her a little closer. *Boy, she does look rough.* "Hey, Girl, don't worry about it. I know for sure that you'll make it. You've got what it takes."

Her smile was lopsided, but she sat up a bit. "Thanks, Tansy. I just wish it were here, already, over and done with."

"I hear you."

Missus McGahon called our attention forward with a pop quiz on yesterday's lecture.

Bryn and I both groaned at the same time. *Not another.* I smiled as I got out a piece of paper.

"Twinkie." Bryn mouthed.

Looking around, other kids were in the same plight, though I bet half of them hadn't fallen off a retaining wall in their wheelchair. That thought set my grin even wider. Bryn cocked a brow at me, but I shook my head. Sometimes there were jokes only a para could understand. Of course, my bestie had been out late looking for me.

An hour later, I propped my chin in my hands and tried to keep my eyelids open during Mr. Teague's monologue in Integrated Computer Applications. Last class before tryouts. I could make it. Whenever I needed a jolt of adrenaline, I looked at the clock. Just watching the hour hand creep towards the four caused my heart to race and my legs to jump spastically though the two weren't connected at all. My hands got clammy, so I wiped them on my skirt. I planned to take it off anyway.

At three fifty-two the bell would ring, but at three forty-five, the teacher dismissed me with a list of computer terms to memorize. I shoved it in the pack with the rest of the miscellaneous papers I'd been given throughout the day and bolted to the restroom. I reapplied deodorant and took the skirt off. It looked like I changed the oil in it, I'd wiped my sweaty palms on it so often. The change gave me the confidence I needed to stop hiding in the restroom and head to the gym.

Heart pounding in my throat, I wheeled towards the gym I'd been to yesterday. Had it been just a day ago that I met Sebastian? My life had changed so much in the last 24 hours it felt like years. Yesterday, I'd honestly showed up only to cheer on Bryn, today I actually planned to try out. Yesterday I'd felt like my life was spinning out of control, today everything seemed so obvious.

The sign on the door read:

Cheer Tryouts here

4:00 pm

When I reached for the door, my backpack vibrated. Dug around and pulled it out.

Mom: Praying for a good tryout. Love

you.

Then it hit me like one of super-sized flyswatter—no matter what happened, whether I made Angel Squad, the Hawkettes game squad, or neither, it didn't matter in the long run. Someone else had a plan. Thank goodness.

Chapter Fifteen

Before I could stall any longer, I opened the door and shoved through. About fifty girls turned to stare at me. Another fifty or so warmed up in uniforms on the far side of the gym and paid yet another girl entering absolutely no attention. It looked like all the girls from both grades had showed up.

I swallowed hard, searching the crowd for a familiar face. A tall redhead broke off from the furthest group and headed my way. Silver bells buried in the fringe on her little white boots chimed with each step. A large black and gold collar swung in unison with her bouncy walk. I imagined all cheerleaders practiced for hours to get in sync with that perfect pony tail swing.

Jealously made my fingers curl into the armrest. An eighth grader, I'd bet. I hadn't seen her in any of my classes. Hopefully not a captain since I'd taken an instant dislike to her. I took a deep breath and rolled to meet her.

She smiled down at me in a way that didn't quite crinkle her eyes. "Hi there, I'm Chrissy." Either she planned to go into public relations, or she was doing that fakey nice thing to the cripple. I chose to think the latter. I had to admit, she made the perfect cheerleader with her wholesome, country-girl good looks.

She spoke loudly too, like my ears were as broken as my spine. It's so hard to train people. "You must be lost. This is cheer tryouts, debate and chess clubs are down the hall a little further."

Okay, so now I couldn't help myself—I rolled my eyes. "Do I look like a chess player?"

That question stopped whatever planned to come out of her mouth next and changed it to an, "Uhhh."

"I'm here for tryouts."

"Uhhh."

I spoke slowly. "This is Cheer, right?"

This simple question seemed to put her brain in gear—finally. "Yes, yes, that's what I said. This is for cheerleaders, or wannabes any way."

"That's me." I moved my chair to roll around her.

She stepped smoothly in front of me so that my

castors stopped an inch from her shin. "What?"

I spoke even more slowly. "Cheerleader. Me. Tryout."

Her eyes narrowed. So maybe Ditz wasn't her middle name. She stepped aside. *She can be taught.* But I could feel her eyes cutting holes in my back like lasers, until a taller version of herself stepped out of the Angel group—a sister maybe?—and called her back to the others. I wheeled up to the crowd, looking for someone I knew. The crowd parted. I realized that they'd been hovering around a table, where Sebastian sat.

He looked up as the quiet broke with whispers and stares in my direction. "Hey, Tansy. Good to see you." He made a check mark next to my name on a pre-printed paper. This started even more whispers. They'd evidently been expecting me. A leg brushed my arm and I turned, expecting the redheaded Chrissy to say something nasty, but she'd returned to the warm-ups far from the wannabes. Bianca stood by my side.

"Hey," I said.

Her smile wobbled and her eyes were bright with tears. "Hey."

Is she going to faint? I reached out and soft slugged her arm like Bryn and I do all the time. "It's going to be okay."

She nodded and leaned closer. "My name's not on the list. Pastor Seb said I could try out, but I have to get my mom's permission if I make team." She swayed on her feet.

"Don't worry about it. You'll do fine. I know it. Unless your Mom doesn't want you to cheer."

She shook her head; that wasn't the case.

"Good then. Just relax. It will be okay."

"You're so calm, even though—" she struggled for a word that wouldn't insult me but said what she wanted to express "—you're different." She ended lamely.

I grinned. "That's me. A different kind of cheerleader." *I hope.* Isn't that what Bryn had called me so long ago when we'd had our first fight? That had only been six days past. But agreeing with Bianca, and making a little bit of fun of myself, seemed to help put her at ease.

Finally, her grin widened, and she didn't seem so tense. "Hey, here's the gang."

Bryn, Isis, and Sarah charged through the gym door. Isis and Sarah had tucked their shirts into their shorts. Bryn wore yoga pants with her shirt tied in a complicated knot at her side. They looked like everyone else in their black bottoms and t-shirts. If I hadn't been permanently attached to this hot pink contraption, I'd fit right in.

The eighth graders split off from the seventh and warmed up in their own corner with stretches and half cheers mimicked from last year's games.

Isis cocked a chin at them, dark eyes flashing. "Showoffs."

Sarah stepped behind her and began a braid in the

other girl's long black hair with quick fingers. Her eyes followed the Angels as they warmed up. "Well, they have a right to be. At least they've seen the Angels perform. We're newbies."

Bryn stepped behind Sarah and finger combed her shoulder length strawberry blonde into a working messy bun. Her own black braids were pulled back into a pony tail with her black and gold scrunchie. The beads at the ends had changed from the purple and blue of the week before to yellow, gold, and ivory—of course.

The Angels stood out from the larger game squad. There were only about ten of them, along with four boys, but they worked together efficiently. They wore their performance gear with long sleeves, bare shoulders and midriffs, and tall black boots. One girl, a tall auburn-haired girl that had called Chrissy over, seemed to call the shots. She walked among the Angels as they stretched and warmed up, straightening a bow here, supporting a walkover there. It took everything I had to tear my eyes away and focus on the things happening closer.

Groups of girls huddled around whispering and talking among themselves. Pastor Seb walked around and checked names on his list. Every time he left a group, the girls grew more animated. Then the scary stuff began—he started calling names. He organized everyone into six groups of ten with one group of four. I got separated from Bryn and put in with Sarah in the smallest group.

I pasted a smile on my face. *Think cheerleader.* I slanted a glance at Chrissy, the redheaded eighth grader. Sure enough, her smile sparkled along with her sky-blue eyes as she kicked to warm up her legs.

"Hi, I'm Tansy." I said to my group

They stared, except for Sarah, but even for a girl who never said much, her nerves obviously prevented her from introducing herself. I jerked my thumb her way. "This is Sarah." She smiled shakily at me, eyes wide. *I hope she doesn't hyperventilate.*

Finally, I got an answer. "I'm Kylie," said a dumpling with blonde hair and cat-green eyes.

"Hanna," said the other. "Why are you here?"

"Trying out—same as you."

She jerked her chin, like she'd say something else, but the door opened and four women filed in. I gulped—the coaches.

Coach Angel stood out as the only one just a little taller than me. The others towered over her. None looked at the girls watching anxiously, simply took a seats behind two tables with three chairs each. Seb handed the checked sheets to his mom who then passed them down. Absolute silence reigned in the gym, except for occasional nervous titter. Even the eighth graders looked a little green.

Finally, Coach Angel stood, her accented English rising and filling the gym easily. "Welcome to cheer tryouts. Today we look for forty *niñas* for two squads.

Coach Kelly and Coach McGahon look for a game squad of twenty-five. Me and Coach Lin look for fifteen. To warm us up, the Angels and the Hawkettes will run through some of last year's routines."

Toni Basil's "Mickey" pounded through the speakers as the Hawkettes ran to the center of the gym in a pyramid shape. Half their number had graduated to high school so just the new eighth graders that had been the newbie seventh graders the year before performed. Still, the shortened routine left those watching on the far side of the gym breathless with excitement and itching to get started. The group I really wanted to see performed next.

The Angels were a smaller, tighter unit. Their routines more dance like and set to a remix that had Bryn bouncing to get started and my hands thumping the push rims. Two boys and girls arced into back handsprings. The boys opening up into pikes halfway through. My mouth dropped open. Eighth graders? They looked like kids off a super cheer squad. My stomach dropped. How in the world would I ever compete with that?

Just three minutes later they finished. But it left me both excited and worried about what was coming next. Coach Angel didn't give me too long to think about it. The music stopped and she walked to center stage. The Hawkettes and Angels arranged themselves on different sides of the gym. Seb moved tables to the stage end. The captains of each group with their co-captains came forward and conferred with the coaches behind Ms. Pereas. I shivered and tried to pay attention to her instructions. *This is it.*

"I will call your names and you will go with the coach I point to. Each group performs, then move to where you are told. Remember, breathe, smile, you are here to have fun, or to convince others to have fun," she said.

A giggle tittered through the groups, but as I looked around, I saw more girls that looked they were going to puke than have fun. The eighth graders seem a little bit better off, but even they looked like their spots weren't assured.

Each coach stood in front of a group. Coach Kelly, also my math teacher, a wide older lady with graying brown hair, headed mine.

"'Kay girls. I want you to follow me." She put her back towards us. Stomp, stomp, stomp, back. Three forward, candlesticks—seemed simple—if you had two legs and two arms. *How in the world?* I took a breath as the coach faced us. "Now you."

The girls lined up with me and I tensed my biceps. I still had no idea how to do this. But I was strong. I grabbed the tires and rock, rock, rock. Bryn's eyes widened at me from a group opposite, she must have thought I was trying to tip over, but I ignored her. I couldn't jump, but every time the girls did a move beyond my skill, I twisted or did something—anything to stay in line. Of course, I couldn't quite keep up, and by the end of the short exercise my lungs screamed for oxygen and sweat trickled down my sides, but I felt good about what I'd managed to do. The other groups finished up, then coach pointed me to the squad under Coach Lin.

She didn't even look at me. She turned her back to us and went right into a routine no way could I copy. Instead, I tried to clap when they did and managed a few turns, but at the last step to the side, a girl I didn't know put her toe under my castor. Before I knew it, three girls crashed at my feet in a tangled mess.

Heat leapt to my cheeks. I had to be stoplight red. Coach Lin pointed back to Coach Kelly. For the next three rotations I bounced between Coach Lin and Coach Kelly. By the third, I wasn't the only one dripping. Coach Angel called a drink break.

While I waited in line, the coaches conferred at the tables. There were a few pointed looks my way, but I pretended to be totally engrossed in the butt of the girl ahead of me.

Bryn tapped my shoulder. "What do you think?"

"Crazy." I tried not to be jealous of her bouncy step. "I think I injured a few people."

She chortled and wiped her glasses on her shirt. "I saw. Don't worry about it. A couple of other girls ran into each other." She perched her glasses back on her nose. "Boy, right now I can see where contacts would be great."

Her lenses fogged immediately, and she went through the whole process again.

"What group are you in?"

"I'm with Coach Angel, but I've been in them all."

Never at the same time as me though. That couldn't be good.

"*Vienen, niñas.*" Coach Angel called. The girls hurried into position. I went back to the group under Coach Lin. The others made sure they started several feet away from my chair.

"No." She pointed to Coach Kelly again. "Over there."

When I got to that group, Coach Kelly pointed back to Coach Lin. "You ended up there."

I tried not to whine, but I knew when I was getting the run around. "She said to come here."

The coach pursed her lips and motioned to a spot a good ten feet away. "Okay, stand there."

Stand?

"Do the routine there."

No doubt about it now. I'd been sidelined.

Chapter Sixteen

For just a second, I wallowed in self-pity. But if I aspired to be a cheerleader, I needed to get the right attitude. A strong hand warmed my shoulder with a squeeze, and I looked up at Pastor Seb. He patted me briefly in passing and gave Coach Lin a clipboard with a fresh sheet of paper.

I shook off the glum that threatened to destroy my day. This was cheer tryouts. Time to cheer. I pasted on a smile and hoped the hotness of my eyes didn't translate to tears. When my group finished the next routine, I clapped. Isis panted on the back row, so I gave her a thumbs up. Her eyes bugged at me, but some of the really nervous girls, the ones that looked like puking, seemed to relax a bit and their wax smiles looked a little more real.

Satisfied that I'd done what I could, I got my first look at Bryn under Coach Angel. Boy, did she look good. She did a back walkover into the splits.

I pumped my fist. "Woot whoo. You go, Girl." My voice reverberated off the walls in a sudden lull as girls caught their breath and waited for the next shuffle.

Bryn grinned at me and leapt to her feet. Coach Angel glanced over her shoulder and frowned. I sank in my chair. Maybe I should tone it down a bit. Mom always said I had a voice that could cure a zombie of his deadness. I don't think she really gets the whole zombie thing. Therefore, I employed my vocal chords to the best of their ability. When I was shuffled to another group and found myself lost in the movements—I stopped. Didn't want to cause another pile up. I clapped or did something to try and keep the energy up.

By the third group, I'd seen just about every single girl come through Coach Lin and Coach Kelly, and I gave them all my best. I didn't get moved though, never made it to Coach Angel. Bryn and I were kept apart. Very suspicious, the way they shuffled her around me, but I never lost track of her, of course. Couldn't miss her. Moves in the other two groups got harder and Coach Lin and Kelly's groups got larger. I got a glimpse of Pastor Seb talking to Bryn earnestly, then next he helped one of the boys spot her in a back flip. She landed it of course.

Finally, Coach Angel motioned all the girls to come together, including me.

"Okay. Now we start the solos." A couple of girls, those with breath to spare, whispered frantically, a few shook their heads. Coach palmed the air. "It doesn't have to be spectacular. I just want to see something that makes you different. If you have a few good gymnastic moves, I want to see. Cheers, dance routines, whatever you want."

Brynley had this covered, for sure. I hadn't had a lot of time to plan, but I had been working on the spins. They'd have to do. The eighth-grade girls and those from the squads the year before, went first. I guess to give us newbies a clue as to what to expect. The four coaches arranged themselves around the tables, the captain and co-captains with them. How much input in the decision making did they really have?

Most every Angel or Hawkette did a round off back handspring. Several did short cheers interspersed with leaps and spins. One or two were real gymnasts that hand-springed the length of the tables. It became obvious why they let these girls go first. Those that had been in cheer before acted like pros, smiles never wavered, staccato cheers bounced off the walls like rifle shots, arms, legs, and backs military straight. Everyone one of them walked with a hand clasped on a wrist behind their backs. Toes pointed. Everything I couldn't do.

Coach Angel checked off the last eighth grader.

"Volunteers from the seventh grade?" Eyes shifted back and forth. I took a deep breath and pushed forward. Might as well get it over with, right? So far no one had been asked to leave. Least I could do was break the ice.

Bryn thumped my arm as I passed. "Go get 'em, Bestie."

Sarah smiled. "You can do it, Tansy."

Bianca twisted her lips into a grimace. "Don't forget to smile."

Even Isis gave me the peace sign.

Their encouragement carried me about three pushes. It felt good to have so many people at my back. I really liked these girls. Boy, I hoped we could all be cheerleaders together. We'd have so much fun.

But before I made it halfway, Coach Lin and Coach Kelly leaned over to Coach Angel. Their arms jerked back and forth, and their voices hissed like they wanted to throw me out before I got my chance.

McGahon, my Texas History teacher, watched me with a slight frown as though expecting me to get out of my chair and do something spectacular. Like this was some sort of equality review she had to pass.

I almost stopped right then and there, then I spied Pastor Seb in his seat behind his mother. He didn't seem to be paying attention at all and a wave of disappointment made my mouth go dry. I gave another push of my chair, letting it roll as I watched him. He sat with his head bent and hands clasped in front of him as his lips moved silently. Is he praying? Here? He looked up at me and gave me a white toothed grin.

My smile grew real. He *had* been praying for me. A sense of peace settled over my jerking heart. Wow, to have courage like that, to just stop and talk to God. Surely that counted for something with the Man, having someone like that in my corner. I'd ask God to help me in tryouts, but I'd left Him at the door instead of bringing Him inside with me. Just like that, I felt His presence all around me. It was as though all the watching eyes and the whispering girls who didn't know me disappeared—including the coaches that didn't like my style.

I stopped in front of the table and met the curious brown eyes of Coach Angel with more confidence than I'd ever felt. The other coaches stopped whispering now that I stood within hearing and sat back, pens poised like lethal injection needles at Huntsville Prison.

Right there, in the two seconds before I came to a complete stop and Coach Angel motioned for me to begin, I let go. "Lord," I whispered in that little corner of my brain that wasn't freaking out. "Whatever happens, I know it's Your plan, and I'm trusting You on this one." Whether I became a cheerleader or not, I would trust Him to know best and where I could make my music count the most. But I planned to give it my best shot, no holds barred.

"Whenever you're ready, Tansy."

I blushed, realizing I'd been staring and smiling while I zoned upwards.

"Oh, thanks." I cleared my throat. Why did my tongue always stick to the roof of my mouth when I needed it most? Better start with some moves.

I jerked my chair from side to side, keeping the big tires still while my castors whirled. I threw it into reverse three feet and stopped. I made candle sticks then threw my fist into the air to form an A. Come on voice, don't fail me now.

"Let's get fired up." I punched the air.

"Get rough." Bow and arrow.

"Get tough." I boxed it up with both arms in a 90-degree angle and shoulder height.

"Get mean." Half T with elbows up and fists clenched in front of my chest.

"Let's get fired up." I punched the air again. "And roll right over that team!" I ended with a touchdown, both arms extended parallel over my head, elbows tight to my ears, fists hard.

Time for the finale. I leaned back, feeling for that perfect balance on the back tires. A couple of coaches gasped. Coach Angel half rose out of her chair. Even Seb jumped up like he planned to come to my rescue—guess my falling off the retaining wall last night spoiled this for him.

I kept smiling and started spinning. One, two,—could

I make it to five? So, what if the world record holder could do eighty in a minute. Sweat beaded and dripped into my eye. Three, four—my arms trembled, already sore muscles now screaming in protest. A low ache started in my back. Five. Six. I dropped down, the world slightly off kilter, and flourished my arms in a big finish. Utter silence magnified my raspy breaths. My hands dangled by the tires. Couldn't move them if I tried.

My chair jerked. Bryn grabbed the push handles and turned me towards the waiting seventh graders.

She leaned over my ear. "That was amazing. You never told me you could do that."

I grinned, trying not to let my disappointment at the lack of reaction to my workout show. "I just learned."

All the other girls had gotten at least a little encouragement from those waiting. Even those that weren't very good. But not a single clap followed me back. No holler or snicker for that matter. Well, that's as good as it got. Maybe it wasn't all that impressive compared to flips and splits, but I felt I'd done my best.

Bryn turned me to face the coaches and stood back. The coaches looked back and forth at each other, like who would be the one to break it to the poor little cripple that she didn't have what they needed. Not that I blamed them. From somewhere behind me, someone started to clap. I twisted in my chair to see who it was, but with my nose at belly button level, I couldn't see beyond the first row.

Then someone else started, Bryn's loud smacks close to my ear.

"Tan-sy, Tan-sy." Isis started the chant I think, and I ducked my head to hide the sudden gush of wetness. Here I thought she didn't like me at all. The beat continued. The whole seventh grade section got into it, stomping and clapping in their own impromptu pep rally.

Coach Angel stood up, motioning for silence. The chanting stuttered to a stop. "We still have many girls to see. Any more volunteers?" Bryn gripped my shoulder and stepped back to the front.

With a cartwheel into a spirit tuck, she started her difficult gymnastics routine. I clapped when she wasn't concentrating and called her name. The others followed my lead. By the time Isis, Sarah, and Bianca went, the seventh graders were out cheering anything the eighth graders had done. At the end, my voice rasped through my tightening throat like a chainsaw and my palms stung. My legs would have hurt too, if I could have felt them because when my hands started to throb, I changed to pounding on my knees.

The last finished with a big smile—who couldn't with everyone chanting and yelling for you? It grew quiet as the coaches once again began to confer. The eighth graders, evidently understanding this would take a while, broke up into little groups, took a drink break, stretched muscles that were beginning to tighten with the cool down. I massaged my legs out of habit and couldn't help smiling. I made it to six spins! Never thought I could, probably couldn't have just a day ago. But with God in my corner, I could do anything.

Chapter Seventeen

I tried not to pay attention to the coaches along with the rest of the girls. Hard to do, especially when arms started waving and the discussion got louder.

I rolled over to the bleachers where Bryn lolled with Isis, Bianca, and Sarah.

I fished out my water and took a long cooling drink and put the necessity bag back on the push handles. I left the book bag for later. Maybe it would disappear. "How long do you think this will take?" I aimed my question at Isis because she seemed to have the inside scoop.

She shrugged. "Don't know."

Bianca jerked her head to the knots of eighth graders.

"Looks like some time. No one's in a hurry to do much."

I nodded and relaxed in my portable chair, glad for some place comfy. I ached all over. The others had to make do on hard, wood bleachers.

A shadow fell across my lap. "Hey, I thought it was really cool what you did."

I looked up into the face of a girl from Computer Class. "Thanks."

Another girl popped out from behind her. "That was cheertastic. We nearly raised the roof."

I laughed at her enthusiasm, agreeing with every word.

She plopped next to Bryn. "I just wish I hadn't fallen in that front hurdler jump. I don't know what happened."

Bryn did her usual understanding thing that made her such a great person to be around. She patted the other's back. "Don't worry about it. That's a tough jump." No kidding, that's one where both feet stand together at the same time, then one goes forward to touch the fists and one leg goes back. "Nobody had a perfect routine, 'cept maybe Tansy, but even she caused a pile up earlier."

It felt good to laugh at myself, and it made the others relax. Pretty soon ten more girls surrounded our original five, each rehashing their routines, bemoaning the bad parts and not so subtlety bragging on the good. Everyone seemed to be encouraging of each other. I just sat back and enjoyed.

It felt really good to be a part of a unit. It never would have occurred to me a few days ago that I'd be sitting in the center of ten or fifteen girls, laughing and having a good time like I was normal. It was becoming clear that it had been me who kept myself separate from everyone besides Bryn these last years. I just didn't know it could feel like this, that I could be accepted as one of them.

Coach McGahon cleared her throat, drawing every eye. "Let me congratulate everyone for a fine job today. It takes a lot of courage to do stand up in front of everyone and give it your all. You all did a super job and let me tell you, choosing the teams was very difficult. If you did not make it, don't be discouraged.

Coach Kelly stood. "I will call the girls who will be on the Hawkette game squad. Please stand on the east wall under the Hawk to receive your collars. After, we go to the stage for a meeting. We do have a pep rally, and football games on top of homecoming coming up."

I smiled nervously at Bryn. She reached for my hand and squeezed so tight my fingers mashed painfully together. After a few shuffles, Coach Kelly started the list started.

Right away Sarah and Isis were called. They ran forward with the others amid cheers, clapping, and not a few jealous looks. At each, the Hawkettes would stomp and clap twice while chanting the new girl's name. The captain stepped forward and draped a black and gold fringed collar around her neck, while the co-captain fastened the back. It all moved fast, smooth, and utterly cool. I *so* wanted to hear my name called, even for the Hawkettes.

Bryn's gripped got tighter, if that was possible, and the tips of my fingers started to go numb and turn blue.

I wiggled them.

She let go. "Sorry."

I tried a smile and know I failed miserably. Bianca peeked from behind the girls remaining. I motioned her over.

She huddled in tight, brown eyes tearing. "I'm not going to get in, I'm not going to make it. I wasn't on the list, now they won't call my name."

I grabbed her hand, making sure not to crush it.

Bryn threw an arm around her shoulder. "*Shhh.* There's still a bunch to go."

But Bianca wasn't the only one in despair. As the group on our side got smaller, and the one on the other got louder. The girls pulled in closer, as though just the sheer presence of bodies could bolster them. I found myself surrounded again, with a tiny peep hole between Bryn and Bianca. Then it was over. The Hawkettes had their girls, all fifty strong. And they were loud, yelling and clapping, stomping, and chanting. They surrounded the newbies, locking them in the center and from my view. I strained to see what was going on, but Coach Angel standing drew my attention.

"Sh, shh, *niñas*. Time for the Angels to be called." I tried to count those left, wanting to figure my chances, but I couldn't get over 11 in the short minute Coach looked over her notes. I knew there were more than that.

"The girls I call, go stand with the Angels. Brynley Winters."

How'd I know she'd be first. I squelched the bite of jealously and whooped. "Woot whoo. You go, Girl."

She leapt forward with a quick grin backwards and headed for her new squad—without me. Fourteen to go.

The Angels surrounded my bestie like a new family. The tall captain stepped forward and clipped a black and gold bow into Bryn's braids. It matched her beads perfectly. How does she do that? Everything was so carefully choreographed it was beautiful to watch.

"Justina Woods, Hadley Carter, Shynia and Shaneka Rhodes." A set of twins ran forward holding hands and shrieking each time a foot hit the ground. Ten to go. With each name called, my heart sunk lower and lower. Would I really not get on after everything that had happened? I'd been so sure. Even though I thought I'd let go and let God take control, told myself I wouldn't be upset no matter what happened, I could feel things tightening inside. Not anger, particularly, but a bone deep disappointment. As though the sadness came from my soul and seeped through me.

"Kyla, Merika, Chrissy." My turn to crush Bianca's fingers, but she squeezed right back, just as hard and worried as I was. "India Adkins, Asera Ramos, Olivia Bolton, Sofia Lopez" Three more. I couldn't stand it. My head was going to pop off with the tension.

"Raven James, Alyssa Little..." Coach consulted her paper again and frowned.

"I can't believe it." I whispered to Bianca. "The very last one and she has to stop."

Bianca's eyes were sad as she looked at me. At least seven girls surrounded us and only one slot remained. Even if one of us did get called, it had to be either her or me. She looked like she was going to faint. "I hope it's you." I surprised myself by meaning it. I looked over to where Bryn stood with the Angels. She wasn't in the middle of everything, she stood to the side where she could watch who was being called. Her eyes met mine, worried behind her glasses. I shook my head, hoping to convey that I'd live. No matter what happened now, everything from here on out had to be magnificent. At least I hoped it would be.

"I'm sorry," the coach apologized as she focused once again on the miserable group of girls left on the far side of the gym. Seb leapt forward with a sheet, as though he'd found what everyone had been looking for and pointed at something for his mother. "Ahh, here it is. Bianca Martinez."

Bianca didn't move. I glanced up at her. Her eyes stretched wide, as though in shock. I shook her hand. "Hey, you made it." Still, no sign of life. I shook harder. "Breathe, Bianca, breathe. You're an Angel. Get going."

Someone behind reached forward and pinched her. Not in a nice way either. Bianca yelped and jumped forward. The Angels laughed a little and waved.

"Come on, Bianca," the captain called. Bianca stumbled a few steps, picking up speed as she went. With Bianca's stalling, I'd totally missed the fact that the last slot had been filled. At least ten girls around me were all that remained in the reject pile. I shrugged. Could have been worse, I could have been sitting out here on my own. That would be embarrassing.

I started to turn and head for the doors. But Coach Angel cleared her throat. "Just a minute girls. After a little discussion with Coach MaGahon, we decided there will be one more girl. We did not call her because, well, she's a different kind of cheerleader."

My heart froze in my chest. That's what Bryn called me, that's what I had embraced as my own. I turned back towards the coaches, slowly, willing my heart to start beating again, willing my breath to move in and out. But just like everything else on my body, it totally ignored my will. Black spots appeared in front of my eyes. *Call the name already.*

"Tansy Fisher. Please come join the Angels." My

breath exploded in the sudden silence. Girls from all sides looked at each other, as though not understanding.

"Wooot whooo!" Bryn bounded forward, screaming at the top of her lungs. She lunged into position on the push handles. I flew across the gym towards the Angels so fast, the captain had to take five steps back or Bryn, not particularly mindful of other people's shins, would have mowed her over.

They closed about me, chanting my name. It started a little weak at first, but it got stronger and fiercer each stomp as my new captain—I really did need to learn her name—stepped forward and clipped that black and gold bow in my hair. I'd made it. I was an Angel.

Finally, my heart started to beat. Gratitude overwhelmed me, gratitude for Bryn, Mom, and Seb, and especially to God for giving me the strength, that I just put my face in my hands and sobbed.

It wasn't some beautiful kind of happy sobbing. Nope, it was flat out, hiccuping heaving sobs complete with running snot. Hands pressed in on my arms, shoulders, Bryn rubbed my back.

"Okay, *niñas*, give her some room." Coach Angel pressed a Kleenex into my hand.

Bodies shifted away, all except Bryn's. *Oh brother, did I really just lose it in front of my Coach? The squad? Everyone?* I hiccuped again and burped. A titter ran through the girls, but it didn't seem to be a mean one, more like they totally sympathized with how I felt. Maybe more than one of them had wanted to breakdown as well, just managed a little more self-control.

"McKenzie," Coach thundered the name of my new captain. "Pass out the practice schedule with the others—we have a pep rally Friday. I'll be there in a minute."

The auburn-haired girl stepped out and motioned for the Angels to join her at the opposite side of the gym as the Hawkettes.

The hubbub lowered to the soft burble of voices, so quiet after the deafening sounds moments before. I wiped my running eyes and nose. "Sorry, Coach."

She remained quiet until I looked up. The roundness of her face belied the sharpness of her eagle eyes that peeled my skin back to reveal the truth underneath. "Tough week, huh?"

I nodded. No way could I explain everything that had happened, least of all the changes inside me.

"You know, Tansy, I wasn't sure if you'd be a good fit for this team. After missing all my homeroom classes, the first week, *and* getting Friday detention—"

Which she'd given to me.

"I think to myself—I don't want that kind of *niña* on my team. Bad influence on my Angels and all."

I swallowed hard and tried to smile, but it didn't work very well—just made me want to go back to sobbing. So, I looked down at my hands before I did. Everything she said was right on. What kind of sane adult would want me on the team after the attitude I'd shown the first few days? "I'm sorry, Coach." *Were those the only words I could think of?* "I'm trying to change, honest."

"I think so, too."

I looked up hopefully.

"After talking to *mi* Sebastian and your *mami,* I think you'll be alright. Trust in God, Tansy. He will help you in all things."

I nodded. "Yes, Ma'am."

Rolling towards the others, Pastor Seb gave me a thumbs up. He tipped the tables on their sides and tucked the legs under. I lifted my chin and smiled, trying to act like I hadn't just fallen apart.

Despite everything, it'd been a good day.

Chapter Eighteen

The anti-climax Friday presented almost boggled my mind. I hardly knew what to do. I actually made it to school—on time. I sat through my classes and had all my homework done. No falling out of bed or off retaining walls. No fresh bruises or cuts. Downright boring after the whirlwind of the last five days.

Of course, Friday detention still loomed over my head, taking me away from the first Angel practice.

For an hour after school, I sat in the library—alone—what other loser would already have detention? It seems that out of five hundred students at Mount Peaceable Junior High, I'd lucked out as the only one. My appointed jailer, Mrs. Blake wasn't particularly happy with me, but what could I say? It'd been a messed-up week. Life in general, however, was looking up.

I watched the clock's big hand inched around the clock face, knowing that each minute meant missed practice time. Coaches hated that, especially if the practice was missed due to detention. Something kind of frowned on by all the other coaches. Cheerleaders needed to keep it clean and because I brought a new layer to the squad with my hot pink chair, I didn't want people thinking I'd be a bad influence on top of it all. Brought in for pity's sake and needing special treatment.

These were the arguments the other coaches could and had used against me. I'd heard them at tryouts when I tried so hard not to listen. I hadn't heard Coach Angel's response, she can be quiet when she wants to be, but it made the other coaches throw up their hands and leave her to deal with me.

She'd told me to meet her in the gym with the others when detention ended. With a pep rally and homecoming coming up, I *needed* to get there ASAP.

"Tansy."

I looked up guiltily at Mrs. Blake's annoyed voice. I'd been tapping the end of my pencil on the desk hoping to force the second hand to move faster. Didn't work. 4:45—15 more minutes. I'd never make it.

"Do your homework."

"I'm finished."

"Study then."

I sighed and opened History. The words blurred. The silent library disappeared and the Angels appeared, pressing in on all sides as the squad ran onto the court at the pep rally. What exactly did Coach Angel have planned? Even in my mind I couldn't see myself with them. Every single one could do a back flip or cartwheel, be part of an aerial— except me that is.

Ugg. I sighed and shifted in my chair. Back in the library. 4:50. Mrs. Blake did her own sigh and finished her grading. Her eyes cut to the clock and I ducked behind my book to hide the grin. She obviously didn't want to be here either.

"I think you can head out, Tansy."

"Yesss." I couldn't help it. I snapped my book shut and tossed it into my backpack.

My jailer frowned, trying to look stern, though she really looked more relieved at getting out of there than angry. "Try to make it to school on time from now on."

I headed for the door. "Yes, Ma'am."

"Tansy?"

I turned back.

"I heard you made the Angels."

I couldn't help the proud smile that statement brought. "Yes, Ma'am."

She stopped, as though she had lots to say, but didn't

really want to have a conversation or hurt my feelings. "Make us proud."

I hesitated in my turn. What did she mean by that? Did the staff worry I'd hold the team back? Everyone knew that each win made our school look better, brought in more money from local sponsors. If this wheelchair didn't go over well at the competitions, it wouldn't just hurt my feelings, it might hurt the whole school. I gulped. I'd never thought much beyond myself and wanting to be a cheerleader. The pinprick of responsibility burst the happy bubble I'd been riding on the last twenty-four hours. Talk about pressure.

I nodded. "Yes, Ma'am," I whispered.

I headed for the gym at a much slower pace than I might have just moments before. Worry clutched at my gut. I'd made the Angels, but would I be the cause of them failing? I shook my head and closed my eyes, seeking confidence God inspired, reassurance this was His plan. Nada. Fear froze my hands on the push rims. Was the high gone already? Was that special feeling of being a part of something greater already gone?

I tried breathing. My heart whispered what my mind wouldn't—a plea for help. In a rush it came when simply asked, that fullness of my heart that I hadn't been abandoned.

"Hey."

I screeched, jumped, and opened my eyes at the

unexpected, but not unknown voice. I looked up to find my castors resting against Pastor Seb's shin. *Really?* Not only did I hold the record for missing homeroom, I was trying to kill everyone. "Sorry."

He smiled. "Actually, I ran into you. Sent by Coach to find you." He leaned down. "I'm warnin' you, she's on a rampage, first practice and all. Now that I've scared you, congrats on making the Angels."

I smiled, but I couldn't keep the expression. "Thanks."

He studied me with chocolate eyes that said too much like his mother's. "Everything okay?"

I nodded, tears threatening to fall at any minute. Wonderful, tardies, a danger to all, and a cry baby. Could my reputation get any worse? I certainly hadn't achieved that cool Angel look I wanted. "Just dandy."

He fell in beside me as I started towards the gym, glad now that Coach didn't expect me until after five. "It can be a little overwhelming sometimes, you know." His voice barely touched the lockers on either side of me it was so soft.

"What?"

"Getting all you want and then learning that wasn't everything it was cracked up to be."

I glared at him. Was he psychic?

He held open the door to the gym and lowered his voice even more. "But don't worry, it's all part of His plan. Remember, He's got you, Tansy."

He gave me a push into the gym full of girls before I could say anything. I looked back at him and his eyes twinkled. No way would I let this go. I whirled my chair and faced him. "How do you know what to say? What people need to hear?"

He cocked his head to the side. "The Holy Spirit. He leads, I open my mouth and things come out." *The Holy Spirit?* There was someone else? He laughed at my obvious confusion. "Get to cheer. I'll see you at Sunday School."

Whoa there. Sunday school? I didn't think I was ready to make a commitment to going to church, but Coach Angel didn't give me time for a response. "Tansy, are you going to join us?"

I spun back and hurried over. "Yes, Ma'am. Sorry."

The other girls seemed to be breaking up, packing drinks and chattering about the new moves they'd learned in the practice I'd missed.

Bryn handed me a paper. "Here's the choreography."

I studied the sheet filled dance moves for a minute. I might as well have turned it upside down, hard to visualize without first having a demonstration. Even so, the translation came through loud and clear this wasn't for me.

Coach Angel waved me over. "*Ven aqui, chica.*" She snatched the paper from my hand. "This is not for you, *me entiendes?*"

"Okay." Like all good Texans, I knew enough

Texican to get the gist of what she meant.

She smiled a secret smile and shooed the rest of the girls away.

Bryn waved her thumbs in the air and mouthed, "text me later."

Coach shook a finger after her. "Go, go. I will talk to Tansy a minute. We all practice together next week." She raised an eyebrow at me—a gleam lit her eyes that had me leaning forward in my chair to catch every accented word. "I have something different in mind for you. You can't enter with handsprings and jumps."

No duh.

"So's I'm thinking darkness and reflective tape." She stood back and studied me and my chair a moment then motioned for Seb. "Come here, *mijo*. Tell me what you think."

Sebastian stopped messing with a basketball and headed over.

"I want some glow in the dark here—" she pointed to my tires "—and here." She motioned to me.

Seb cocked his head from side to side. "I think a type of duct tape might work." He paced around my ride.

Is this how a mannequin feels? I wondered.

"What do you want to show?"

"Spins definitely..." As she continued plotting, my hopes rose. She wasn't going to make me try and do the things like the others. I shook my head. I'd already stopped trusting. I should have known God had everything worked out. Every time I doubted, even the little things, somehow things worked out, especially when I just let go and trusted. I wasn't like the others, and Coach Angel knew that. I planned to be the best different kind of cheerleader there could be.

Chapter Nineteen

The celebration party took place that Saturday night. Leo pushed me across the highway and down to the Links where we used to live. I tried not to look at the bright red door of our old house but couldn't help it. No one lived there anymore. With the industries around Mount Peaceable laying off so many workers, many houses lay empty. Mine included.

Like a suspended time capsule, it crouched above the overgrown concrete drive and dead lawn. It seemed to wait for me and my family to step back into our old lives. Poor house. It didn't know it'd been abandoned. I wanted to explain what had happened, but that seemed foolish.

Instead, I turned my eyes away from the dead privet bushes and the yard I'd played in for eight years.

Leo didn't look either. Just pushed me up to the house next door, rang the bell, and headed back home without a word. He hunched his shoulders and pulled his cap down over his eyes as he passed the deserted house, and it wasn't due to the glaring sun.

He looked lonely.

I didn't want to let go of the closeness I'd felt with him the night he'd fixed my ride. Even if it'd only been a silly old pecan stuck up in the tire. "Bye." I just wanted to let him know I understood the painful memories coming here stirred, and that he wasn't alone.

He turned as though surprised and gave me shrug. It could have been my imagination, but he seemed to walk taller.

Bryn threw open the green door. "Party." Her shriek made me jump and nearly burst my eardrum. "Get in here. Everyone's here already."

I wheeled into the cool foyer then on to where a muted music pounded from the kitchen—Christian, I'm sure. Isis, Bianca, and Sarah picked through cartons of ice cream overflowing the black granite of the center island. A sugar crush of multi-hued sprinkles, chocolate chips, Gummie Bears®, ButterFinger® crumbles and a rainbow of syrups peeked from behind sherbets, frozen yogurt, and ice cream cartons.

The others stared in wide-eyed delight. I, however, knew that one of the things Mrs. Winters did well was throw a party—and dug right in. I rolled right up to my usual spot—yes, I have one in her house too—and reached for the scoop. Never mind everything sat at nose level.

Ah ha—white chocolate raspberry swirl—my favorite. Mrs. Winters hid out in her bedroom to give us girls some room. I had to admit, she's cool that way. Streamers of black and gold hung from the pot rack. Helium balloons and rosettes rose from the corners of the island. Party plates, spoons, and napkins, all in our school colors, completed the pretty picture. Bryn had been busy.

I took my time—not often did I have such a great creation selection. Two perfectly round scoops of the swirl and one plain chocolate right in the middle. Drizzle with butterscotch, sprinkles, and perch Mr. Gummi at the top.

I sat back and admired it. "Perfection."

Sarah giggled and added a tiny dollop of whipped cream to the bear's head for a darling little cap. "Now he's perfect."

I stared at her. "You've got the gift."

Bryn rolled her eyes. "Tansy thinks food is art. I just eat it."

Isis took a big bite of cookies and cream (how boring is that) slathered with chocolate syrup and chocolate chips. "I agree."

Bianca seemed to be just staring in amazement.

Bryn's house is kind of overwhelming, all spacious and decorated with ideas straight off HGTV.

I waved a hand in front of her nose. "Eat. Party time." Maybe she just zoned out occasionally.

Bryn tapped her bowl with her spoon in a tinkly attention getter. She cleared her throat and looked down her nose at us for half a second, then she burst into giggles. "Okay cheergirls. Now that Tansy has her ice cream." I saluted her with my spoon. She grinned back. "Here's to making it."

The girls, including me, hooted and hollered.

Bryn cleared her throat and continued. "I'm so glad we all got onto a squad—that no one got left out. Especially you, Tansy." I ducked my head. *Enough with the tears already.* My bestie's the best. "I'm glad you didn't let go of your dream."

I sniffed. "Stop it. This is a good time." I looked around this great group of girls. My heart soared to see not a single eye without the shine of happy tears. Something prodded my gut. "I'm just glad you never let me give up, Bryn. You and God just kept poking at me." I stared into her almost black eyes. "I need to say I'm sorry for being such a jerk. And thanks." There. I'd said it what had needed to be said all week. She'd been right all along. Time for her to rub it in. But she was Bryn, my best friend.

She just smiled wider—that shark smile that crinkled her eyes that let me know I might be getting some payback, but it'd be the fun kind. Isis' unladylike snort made my head turn. The timing, the look in her eye, everything, reminded me of me just a few days before. I sat back with my dish and studied her. She was the only one, besides me, who had not been to church camp with Bryn.

Suddenly, I saw her with a heart that understood the frustration that popped up whenever anyone gave credit to God. Hadn't I just been there? Hadn't I been the one to throw a Bible on the ground? Hadn't I picked a fight with my best friend over her relationship with Jesus? Isis refused to look at anyone, merely shoveled in another heaping bite.

As my new friends chattered about tryouts and the last practice, I realized I needed to tell people about God. Others like me needed to have the relief and peace that I had found just overnight, and I didn't even know much. I needed to learn more, how to tell people in the right way. People like Isis, who were uncomfortable around talk of God. Meg.

Seb had invited me to Sunday school, I had to go and ask him. How did it all come together so smoothly? Bryn, Seb, the angel, everything? How did that happen to other people?

"Hey Tansy, are you with us?"

I smiled at Bryn. "Sure."

"So, what happened after we left practice? Coach sure wanted you all to herself."

I took a big bite of my creation and closed my eyes in bliss—drawing it out as long as I could.

"Taan—sy." Bryn complained.

I gave her an ice cream grin. "It's going to be so cool. Different than anything I've seen, even on TV."

Bryn motioned to the table in the morning nook. "Over here, over here." She pushed me over knowing I wouldn't let go of my food. I love ice cream.

"Seb's got this glow-in-the-dark duct tape."

"Oh, yeah," cut in Isis, "I used it for a book cover last year-its glows bright green in the dark."

I nodded. "Right. That's the stuff." I glared at Sarah and Isis. "Remember, this goes no further than our group, I think Coach wants it as a surprise next Friday." Wide-eyed they nodded. "Anyway, they're going to put it all over my ride and my uniform, so I'll look like a stick figure in a wheelchair."

Bryn's eyes practically glowed like the tape in question. "That sounds so cool. I can't believe you didn't text me last night."

I flushed. I'd been so worn out I'd only managed dinner, a quick shower, and bed. I'm sure I drooled, I'd been so out of it. "Sorry about that."

She shook her spoon at me. "Never again, ya hear me."

"I'll try."

"So, will the Angels be glowing too?" asked Sarah

shyly.

I shook my head. "Just me and whoever is going to cartwheel in at the opening. It would be so cool if it were you or Bianca."

"Then what?" Isis prodded.

"Then the Angels do their thing."

Isis leaned back. "It's so cool you guys have boys on your team."

Bryn wrinkled her nose. "Four is all. Pastor Seb works mostly with them. They're just bases and stuff."

"They can sure spring around." Bianca finally came out of her zone and joined in.

"Of course, they can, they're from the Gymnastics school," said Sarah shyly. They were eighth graders and I hadn't been to a practice yet, so I hadn't even learned their names, let alone talked to them.

She waved her hand airily. "Michael and Zane are in my Sunday School class."

"Too bad it's not Jyme or Jamie." Isis teased, but her voice had a hard note to it that made me look at her sharply instead of flushing like maybe I should have. It was obvious now, every time church or God came up, Isis turned into a spoil sport.

I didn't want to draw attention to her by asking about her problem. That would just make her angry—I should know. Seb would be able to tell me what I needed to do.

Sunday School was a blast. Under Pastor Seb's direction, some older teens put on a skit about a deaf cat and all the misunderstanding he had with his friend Dog until Jesus healed him. I laughed so hard I cried. Then came lots of music. The woman that sang the night of back-to-school bash, led out. I felt self-conscious about singing with someone like that. Beside me Bryn belted out the words as they appeared on the screen and soon enough, I joined in.

The kinship I'd felt with my little group of girls was nothing compared to sixty kids, all of the same heart, singing and swaying as one. It was awesome.

Then Sebastian went into pastor mode and preached like a hellfire evangelist I'd seen in movies. But his sermon didn't talk about going below, no, he talked about love and forgiveness and sharing.

He got mobbed by kids afterwards, as though he were a rock star. I hung out in the back, waiting to see if I could get a minute with him. Bryn disappeared to find her Mom when the adult study group let out, so I was left alone to watch.

How'd he draw people to him like that? Just watching him I wanted to go closer. His voice rose and fell like the songs we'd sung earlier. I heard things like "I'll pray for you" and "Let me see what I can do to help". Sometimes he just gave out hugs. Some kids, like me, hung out in the back, wanting to talk, but maybe had more personal things to say they didn't want others to hear. The more I waited, the more unsure I became. Who was I to think that I could tell others about God like he did? It seemed to come to him naturally, where I had no clue as to what to do.

Just as the doubts made me grab the push rims and turn away, Seb hugged his last follower and reached out to stop me.

"Hey, Tansy."

I froze.

"I'm glad you made it today. You seemed a little shocked the other day."

I smiled a little. "I guess I hadn't thought too far ahead. It's all so new." I couldn't meet his eyes, couldn't get my thoughts in order to tell him about my friends and how I wanted to share with them like he did.

He knelt in front of my chair. "What is it?"

Almost on their own the words tumbled out. "I have friends, who don't know God and the music and Meg slit her wrists and I want to help but I don't know how."

"Whoa, whoa, slow down."

I gulped for a breath. "I just don't think I know enough. I don't know enough to do—" I looked away from his questioning eyes. "What you do? I don't know what to say."

"You get to know Him, Tansy, and the more you

know Him, the more you can tell others. Let the Holy Spirit work in your life, people will see the changes in you, and they will ask."

"Meg won't."

"The one who cut her wrists?"

I nodded.

He chewed his lip. "Sometimes you have to step out in faith, Tansy, take the plunge. Even if you're rejected, you may plant a seed that, given time, will sprout and blossom."

I nodded. "Okay." I hoped that God's presence was already showing my life, but now it was obvious. I needed to go see Meg.

Chapter Twenty

The music thumped from under the gym doors, around the corner and to where I sat in the girl's bathroom with Coach Angel crouched in front of me. I donned a hoodie lined with the glow tape and sweat pants over my leggings lined with the stuff. The problem was, the tape didn't want to stay stuck to the chair.

Although the Angels had practiced all week on the moves for today's pep rally, this was the first time we'd used the tape. My head snapped up as the music changed. The Hawkettes presented their routines now, then the football team would be introduced, then the Angels. I swallowed hard, trying to sit still when the only thing I wanted to do wheel out of the building screaming. The other Angels already sat on the front row, ready, except for me and Bryn.

My bestie sat on the sink doing her freaky "absolutely still" thing. After a few minutes I began to suspect it was fear that froze her in place.

"Breathe, *niñas*." Coach smiled as she finished fiddling with the tape and stood. "I think it will hold." She reached over and adjusted my hood. "Let's get out there."

Bryn leapt down and grabbed the push handles, her breath whooshed in my ear. Sweat broke out on my brow and I wanted to blame it on the clothing, but I knew I'd be hot in anything.

"We've got this," she chanted. "We've got this, we've got this."

I couldn't see her around my hoodie, but I'd nodded. I said a quick prayer. So glad that I could talk to God whenever I needed. It became easier each time I did it, too. Lately it seemed like all the time, but at least my best friend assured me she did it too. Especially in times like this.

The music hit me like a physical wall as coach opened a side door and peeked in. "Soon."

I got a glimpse of a sea of apathetic faces and a line of football players looking tiny in their heavy gear. Someone in a fuzzy black and gold Hawk outfit swooped in front of bleachers filled with black shirts. Co-coach

McGahon sat with the Angels, her hand motioned to Mckenzie to get the girls ready.

Coach Angel touched my shoulder, then waved for Bryn to follow her through the halls to other side of the gym. Seb appeared and I sighed, glad I hadn't been left alone.

He grinned. "Ready?"

"As ready as I get."

He peered through the steamed glass. "Okay. Paul's getting the lights." He grabbed the door handle. "On my mark."

I held my breath. The dance remix beat out the melody the squad had practiced to all week. Seb's eagle tattoo waved as he counted under his breath. "One, two, now."

He pulled open the door.

I didn't hesitate. I wheeled in. Darkness covered the gym, broken only by the six crimson exit signs. A stick figure bobbed at the other end. Bryn. I searched for my mark, glow tape stuck to the floor where the bleachers began. Finally, the bright marks came into focus, right as my cue came in the throb of the song.

I shot towards the blur of movement that was my friend, being careful to stay just a foot to the right for her part of the routine. Count—one, two, three, four, five. Stop. Bryn's stick figure lunged towards me in a cartwheel and I began to spin. Counting again. One, two, three, four, five, six. I stopped as the lights flared to life, flourishing my hands above my head.

I didn't have to look behind me to know that the Angels were in position at just the right time, because the music changed and I pushed to the opposite end of the Angel formation, watching with pride as the group jumped into action.

The darkness seemed to have brought the kids in the stands to life, and with the different music several jumped to their feet. Some stomped in time with the beat. I didn't have much time to watch. I needed to prepare for my next cue.

The front row of Angels, Bryn, now shed of her hot hoodie, McKenzie, Tanika, and Paige, rolled on their backs, legs waving straight and tall, the middle row stepped left, last row went right, pony tails flying in a head toss. Coach Angel caught my eye and motioned with her chin. I wheeled out center stage in front of the Angels and everyone.

Bryn and Mckenzie crowded close. Two smaller girls, Emma and Yanine, who looked like they should still be in fifth grade, put one foot on their knees and one foot on my arm rests, standing in a short pyramid. I grabbed ankles to help steady their feet on the surface slick from my sweaty palms. The boys cartwheeled and then opened up into flat pikes in front of it all. Without looking, I knew that in the back the aerials were taking flight, landing safely into the

arms of their team mates while Seb and the coaches
spotted from the back.

I felt the disaster begin, but it happened before I knew
how to stop it. The little girl on my left, Emma, shifted for
her dismount just a split second before the one on my right.
I let go of her ankle. She pushed off as Yanine put her
whole weight on the armrest for her own departure. As
light as the two of them were, it was enough to tilt my
chair.

To catch herself, Yanine pushed harder, giving me a
good shove into Bryn, in the process of rising from her
knees. For the second time that month, I found myself
falling.

Bryn and I tumbled in a mass of waving arms, chair,
legs. My ride landed on Bryn, spilling me out like a bag of
garbage. My head thumped hard on the shiny wood floor.
Black and white polka dots danced in front of my eyes.
The music ended abruptly.

I blinked, trying to focus. Something wet trickled
down my lip. *Oh brother, I hope I'm not crying in front of
everyone again.*

I touched my hand to my face. It came back red.
"Bryn, you okay?"

I couldn't see her through the faces surrounding me. I
pushed them away. My chair clanked somewhere behind
the helpers. Seb reached through the crowd, Coaches
Angel and McGahon with him. Together they crouched

around me like football players in a huddle.

Someone pressed a napkin into my hand. Coach Angel's no-nonsense voice cut into my confusion. "Your nose is bleeding, *Niña*. Sit still. You banged your head good."

"My legs." I motioned. "I need to—" They backed off and faces blanched. Para legs tend wrap and tangle like bits of loose string if allowed to, unlike regular legs with nerves that scream "don't go there." It's weird looking until you get used to it. Obviously, these people hadn't seen legs tangled before.

"Does it hurt? Do you need help?"

I didn't know all those answers yet, so I waved away more hands and grabbed the sweat pants, pulling the right leg over the other until I sat in a more natural position.

Bryn pushed my chair forward and I smiled. She seemed unharmed.

Seb leaned down. "Okay, Girl, you know the drill. I've only got one arm, you know." *Like that stops him from doing anything.*

I reached up and grasped around his neck. His arm snaked under my knees and his stump steadied my back.

He deposited me in my ride as easy as could be. "Good to go?"

I looked up and nodded, holding the napkin to my nose. "No problem. Not like falling off a retaining wall or anything."

"'Atta girl."

The coaches finally backed away. It seemed as though everyone in the bleachers had been holding their breath and let it out all at once. Whispers started that bounced up into talking. Then the fingers started to point. I'd become what I never wanted, a freak show. Necks craned, wide eyes in curious faces. Kids turned to each other as though to ask—where's the blood? A cripple just fell out of her chair. We want more.

The Angels surrounded me, cutting out the faces. Bryn hugged me.

McKenzie started it, I think, a chant among the squad, low at first and then rising. "Tan-sy, Tan-sy."

I flushed and ducked, shaking my head. "Stop that. I'm okay." This wasn't like tryouts where just us girls formed a close-knit group, this was the whole school. Heat scalded my cheeks. I hid my face in the bloody napkin.

But they didn't stop. "Tan-sy, Tan-sy."

Feathers brushed my cheek. I looked up, the mascot swooped from side to side between the Angels and bleachers again. This time, a voice come out of the chipped yellow fiberglass beak. "Tan-sy, Tan-sy."

I knew that voice. I narrowed my eyes at the felt and fake furred bird as it danced by. "Jamie?"

The Hawk put a wing to its beak to shush me.

The student body took up the cheer. "Tan-sy, Tan-sy."

Seb leaned down close. "Perfect time to make your

escape." He motioned to Bryn. "Better let the two wounded warriors lead."

Bryn quickly took up position at the push handles, but not before I saw a big scrape on her leg where the hub of my tire must have caught her.

"Your leg."

She patted my shoulder as she pushed me to the door. "It's okay, just a scratch."

The Angels fell in line behind. I craned my neck to see. McKenzie led, her arms clasp behind her back. The Angels marched out of the gym in style.

Safe on the other side of the door Coach Angel let out a sigh. "Well, Tansy, you sure know how to get a crowd going don't you."

I looked down at my hands. "I'm sorry. I don't know what happened."

"It's okay. We'll get it right."

"Oh no, you won't."

I jerked my head at the deep voice I'd only heard a few times before. Principle Ford.

Coach Angel placed herself between us and the big man. The Principal had played football back in college and still had the big muscles and no-neck look of a player. She looked like a mouse in front of a bull.

"There will be no more of this. This whole routine is a liability for our school. If I'd known what you'd planned I would have put a stop to it last week. This is unacceptable."

Coach Angel looked at me and the rest of the Angels huddled behind her. "This is not the place. Let's talk in your office. After I take care of my squad."

Mr. Ford stepped back. "In my office after school." He hurried back into the gym. A few seconds later I heard his voice on the speakers, moving the pep rally into its final moments with an announcement for the football game the next day.

Coach let out a breath. "Okay, *niñas*. Time to decompress. Great job, everyone. Things like this happen and it's best to get the kinks worked out now. Change out of your uniforms and hang them up. You want them to stay nice." She touched my shoulder. "How's your head?"

"I'm fine." *Definitely not the time to look like a wimp.*

I turned with the others but couldn't figure out how to keep the napkin on my nose and push at the same time. Bryn shuffled back. The light of the performance had gone out of her eyes and she looked like I felt, like she'd spent all day at Six Flags standing in line with only three 5-minute rides to show for it.

My head ached and my nose felt stuffy, but I didn't pay any attention. Mr. Ford's tone worried me more. *Something* would happen at that meeting between him and Coach Angel and I knew I wasn't going to like it.

A dullness hung over me the rest of the day. I went through the motions, pulled off the hoodie and sweats, folded them neatly and placed them in the pile in the restroom under McKenzie's watchful eye.

Bryn pulled at the tape on a tire. "Do you want some help getting this off?"

I lifted a shoulder. "Leave it. I like it." It could be the last time I got to do anything like this. I wanted it to last. She nodded and helped me maneuver through the door.

The silence between us lasted the whole ride home. Mrs. Winters tried to get the conversation started, but neither Bryn nor I wanted to talk. Even Leo must have sensed it when the cherry colored van stopped to pick him up, because he climbed in quietly and didn't ask the questions that seemed to leap in his dark eyes.

Bryn's family usually did a Friday night dinner in town, so Mrs. Winters dropped off Leo and me and headed out right away. I lifted my hand at Bryn. I wondered how the meeting between Coach Angel and Mr. Ford was going. Would she fight for me? Or had my cheerleading career ended before it'd even begun.

Instead of going in, Leo grumbled something and tossed his books onto the ramp. He headed over to the gaping hole in the siding at sat down beside it.

I wheeled over. "Whatcha doing?"

He righted one of the panels. "I'm sick of this house

looking like a dump." He snapped it into place.

"Cool."

In just a few minutes he had all three righted. I pushed backwards and nodded. "Much better. I always hated how it grinned at me like a jack-o-lantern."

Leo glanced at me from under his cap. "Yeah, me too." Once again that closeness I'd felt with him last week wrapped around me and it made me smile, despite the impending doom the principal's meeting forecast.

"You're a handy man, you know it? Just like Dad."

Leo glared at me and stomped towards the ramp. "I'm nothing like Dad." Boom. Good feeling gone. He slammed through the door, leaving me staring into nothing.

With a whoosh, the wind whipped down the street. Leaves and trash skittered across the pavement. I eyed the sky. Dark clouds rushed about, and the trees bent in the onslaught of a cloud front. I grabbed the push rims and hurried into the trailer as the rain thundered down.

Chapter Twenty-One

My heart told me I needed to go see Meg. I didn't want to, but the relief and the peace that filled me wanted to overflow and it actually hurt me to think of the pain that drove her to slit her wrists. Even with the knowledge that my cheerleading hung on a slim thread.

Deep down I knew that if Jesus hadn't have found me and kept trying to get my attention, in a few years I might have found myself exactly where she was. Alone in a hospital bed, knowing no way to loosen those knots, no way to get rid of the pain.

But now, I felt so light I could nearly levitate right out of my chair. Of, course, I'd had the weekend to think about it. To let go of the crushing worry and pray that God just take control. Everything seemed to work out better that way.

But this Sunday afternoon, it pressed on me as important that I let Meg in on this secret. I now knew why Bryn couldn't keep her joy to herself, it bubbled and burbled like a spring persistently pushed through dirt and stone until it burst into the light of the surface. I wanted to shout that I'd been saved from the mountains—or at least the highest hill in Texas which, incidentally, isn't Mount Peaceable but Guadalupe Peak in Western Texas where there are actually mountains.

But then again. Meg frightened me. I knew exactly how angry I'd been. To think of myself ten times worse was scary. And that's how I thought of Meg. I thought long and hard on how to approach her. What worked best for me? God had thrown people at me. Strong Christians like Bryn, Sebastian, and Coach Angel. He'd even put an angel in the mix.

It almost made me giddy to think that I could be one of those people. That an encounter with little old me might be the stepping stone across the pain to Jesus. But this was Meg I was going to see. I mean, come on, she had the strength of despair to slit her own wrists. The anger and desperation that drove her to do that froze every joy within me. Compared to the dragon inside her, my worry had been a lizard.

I shook my head at myself. Doubt again. Every time I let it get the best of me, God proved me wrong. Of course, *He* could deal with Meg. Sebastian had told me he just let the Holy Spirit lead—I still wasn't sure on that—but I certainly could stand back and let God do His Great Plan Thing. I'm just the instrument after all.

So, I'd headed to the book store and found the most brilliant Bible I could. Like mine, it was covered in sparkles and gems, but this one was rainbow colored. I smiled as I tucked it into a matching bag with metallic tissue papers in rainbow colors. Bryn would be so proud of me.

Mom glanced at me. "You ready?"

I sat frozen in the front seat for five minutes while the car idled in front of the hospital. *You can do this. You can.* I breathed out slowly and closed my eyes. I focused and said a quick prayer. A little self-conscious with Mom watching so closely. "Yeah." *No.*

"Do you want me to go with you?'

Yes! "No. I can do this."

"Room 325."

I nodded. "Got it."

Mom got out to get the chair. Guess we couldn't sit and block the handicap ramp any longer. In only a few quick pushes, I set my brakes in the elevator going up with an old lady that smelled like lavender and watched me like a hawk. Probably because I looked like I could puke any time.

With every second, my heart beat harder. Surely the other passenger could hear it. But she got off on the second floor with a smile that told me she wanted to pat me on the head. I gritted my teeth. I hate hospitals.

My phone beeped.

Bestie: You do it?

Trust her to keep tabs on me.

Me: Headed up.

Of course, I'd run this whole visit idea by Bryn earlier. She'd offered to come along, but I'd thought it best to go alone. At least Meg kind of knew me. Well, we saw each other once or twice a week—if that counted. I hoped it did.

Bestie: I know you can do it.

Me: I hope so.

The elevator dinged. By the time the door opened, my hands shook where they gripped the wheels. I hadn't worn my gloves so my first shove on the push rims had no grip and I didn't move. A nurse looked up from the station and stared. Clearing my throat, I tried again and was relieved as the chair sailed forward.

A young blonde lady in blinding pink scrubs and heavy black mascara stood up and padded over in her silent nurse shoes. "Can I help you, Honey?"

I studied the number plaques on each hallway and bit back a snarky response. Most likely I knew this hospital better than she. She seemed fresh out of school, pretty young, I'd probably been coming here longer than she'd had a job.

I immediately felt sorry and tried to smile. "I'm looking for Meg Barnes. #325."

The nurse's face changed, and she nodded knowingly, as though the fact that I too was in a wheelchair explained it all. Of course, it could have been the present on my lap.

I followed her without a word. Best not to say anything than let my mouth pop off with something I'd regret. *Boy, I don't know if I have the energy for this.* I'd to end up biting my tongue off for sure, but I just can't stand condescending adults.

My helpful guide stopped at a door two down from the nurses' station. I could have found it on my own. Maybe the nurse was bored, and I'd made her day. I tried to smile, but it left my face almost as quickly as it began. The heavy wooden panel loomed in front of me like a castle gate, huge and unyielding. It was shut firmly, and I could tell if hospitals had locks, it would have been.

There are varying degrees of closed doors in a recovery wing. I knew and had used them all at some point in my own rehabilitation. There's the wide open, come on in that desperately lonely people do. There's the half closed, I'm watching TV and want a little privacy, but you're welcome to come break up the rerun of *As the World Turns* if you want to (which is really addicting no matter what age you are—trust me). There's a slight crack that invites a knock before entrance. The invalid may be in the middle of a good book or an enema—don't want to walk in on that one unprepared. But there was no crack in Meg's. No pinprick of light. That screamed STAY OUT better than any sign.

I tapped softly. Immediately a TV began playing. I knocked harder. *Two could play at this game.* The volume got louder. I slammed my open palm on the door. "Meg, it's Tansy from PT."

The TV *snicked* off. An invitation. I gave the door a push.

Curtains tried to keep out the late afternoon sun. But it didn't work. The nostril searing disinfectant smelling room contained two beds. Meg occupied the furthermost from the door, as though she'd put herself into a corner.

She watched me, waiting.

"Hi."

She nodded. Oh. It was that way was it. I tried to feel superior, but I could see me in everything she did, and I knew I'd moved past that. Well, mostly. "I brought you a present." I set it on her lap.

She dug through the paper, the white bandages on her wrists flashing. She frowned as the little bit of sunshine creeping through the curtains illuminated the sparkles. Tiny reflections danced on her face. For just a moment they wiped away the bruises under her eyes, filled her pale cheeks with raspberries and put a twinkle in her eye.

"A Bible?"

I hurried to explain. "Believe me, I know you think it's the lamest gift. I got one too, but it helped me find my music." I fumbled for words, aware of her dark eyes studying me like a bug. "I thought, maybe it could help you find some answers." Still she said nothing. "If anything, you can make pretty designs on the wall."

That made her smile. "What do you mean about the music? You play or something?"

That's all I needed. I scooted closer. "It's something Keryn told me. Wanna hear?"

She nodded in a wobbly way. Like she'd heard lots of stories over the past few days—and I'm sure she had. People liked to dig up all kinds of inspirational "this happened to me too" to make you feel better. I *knew* mine was different. God could change her life if she would just let Him. I couldn't make her, but I could tell her my take on the whole "I'm an angry paraplegic" thing and give her something to think about.

"Well, it's like this—you know how I always wanted to be a cheerleader? Well, the other day..."

I closed Meg's door quietly, relieved to have it over with. I rested my head back and took a deep breath. My phone beeped.

PastorSeb: Good news!

Then nothing. I was so not in the mood to play guessing games.

Me: ???

PastorSeb: Congratulations. You're officially a cheerleader again. ☺

Joy warred with the relief in my soul. Coach Angel had done it. Somehow, she'd convinced the principal I should be on the team. I started down the hall, not sure which was the best feeling. Being back on the squad or knowing that with my visit I might have given Meg a chance at the happiness and peace within me.

I poked the elevator button. Seeing I had a few floors before it arrived and no one was around, I bowed my head for a quick prayer.

I prayed my visit would make a difference. I thanked God for the faith He and others had in me. When I looked up at the elevator chime, my heart thrummed in my chest, a slow beat with definite cheer overtones, the beginning of a new melody. My song.

Meg watched the door snick shut after Tansy, leaving her isolated in her room—again. She stared after her little friend long after she had gone, not seeing the walnut colored door, but Tansy in physical therapy, working harder than anyone, wanting so much to be something people never thought she'd be. And look at her now, she'd made the cheer squad, not just any cheerleader, but the Angels.

Good for her.

Meg shook her head, shaking loose the sparkles of joy that tried to cling to the cobwebs of pain in her head. Joy had no place here. Reflexively, she pushed the long-sleeved hospital gown up her arm, ignoring the fresh bandages to study the fine scars that climbed her left forearm and onto the bicep.

Tiny scars, some no bigger than a fingernail, opalescent against her porcelain skin. A cut for each hurt, a letting of the pain inside. Some were large, one for when her parents split, another for her boyfriend leaving, she touched the one for the accident that left her a paraplegic. She knew them all. The shunning of her new friends, her mom's creepy new boyfriend, her dad's remarriage.

Not today. Today wasn't good. Tomorrow couldn't be better, no matter what Tansy said. Her fingers moved from touching the scars to stroke the jewel encrusted covering of her gift, tracing the words Holy Bible. It seemed to soothe her like touching the scars hadn't. Tansy had told her a story of anger and demons, of need—but what of despair?

Again, Meg shook herself and flicked on the TV, letting it drone as her mind drifted into the blackness the pain brought, ignoring the knocking at her soul, questions Tansy raised about her own life. Questions. Knocking. Questions. Knocking.

Songs for reading
A Different Kind of Cheerleader.

- "Wake me up" Avicii

- "I Will not be moved" Natalie Grant

- "Blessings" Laura Story

- "Whom Shall I Fear" Chris Tomlin

- "People Like Us" Kelly Clarkson

- "You Raise Me Up." Josh Groban

- "10,000 Reasons" Matt Redman

- "One Thing Remains" Passion featuring Kristian
  Stanfill

- "You are More" Tenth Avenue North

- "You Love Me Anyway" Sidewalk Prophets

- "What if" Nichole Nordeman (Tansy's Song)

- "I Will Rise" Chris Tomlin

Reading Guide
for
A Different Kind of Cheerleader.

What character in the story do you identify with or enjoy the most? What are the character's strengths or flaws that draw you?

Tansy feels that God was to blame for the difficulties in her life. Discuss how her attitude changes and the key scenes that bring these changes about.

What kind of friend is Tansy to Bryn? Is Tansy a friend you would have chosen to have? Discuss the differences in the two girls and how they went about being a friend. Was Bryn wrong to keep bringing up God when she knew it made Tansy angry?

Tansy feels that the man in the cemetery was an angel. Do you think so? Why or why not?

Would you want Tansy on your cheer squad? Do you think Coach Angel or Principal Ford was right? Why?

Tansy thinks her injury defines her. Does it really? How did her encounter with Sebastian change her view? Do people look at others and judge them based on what they see instead of what is in their hearts? How does God change the way we see ourselves and others?

Discuss the role music played in the softening of Tansy's heart.

At the end of the book, Tansy decides to visit Meg. Discuss the gift she took. Would you have done the same? Why or why not?

Other Books by Lira:

A Different Kind of Black Belt
Forests for the Children
Daddy-lion Wishes
Hotshot Romance

Want to learn more about Lira and what's coming next?

http://www.lirabrannon.com/

http://www.adifferentkindofcheerleader.com/

http://www.pinterest.com/lirabrannon/

https://twitter.com/Lislann

https://www.facebook.com/LBrannonAuthor

www.ingramcontent.com/pod-product-compliance
Lightning Source LLC
Chambersburg PA
CBHW021030130626
46552CB00005B/1769